A flashing paw tipped with razor claws swiped at Fargo's throat. He barely got the Henry up in time to block. The force made him stagger. Regaining his balance, he went to fire.

Crouching, the jaguar hissed at the old man and then came at Fargo in a rush. A forepaw caught the Henry's muzzle and a claw must have hooked the sight because the next moment the rifle was torn from Fargo's grasp.

Fargo stabbed for his Colt. He was clearing leather when the jaguar slammed into him like a fur-clad avalanche. The impact bowled him over and he wound up on his back with the big cat astride his chest. Glistening fangs were poised over his face. He tried to draw, but his arm was pinned. The cat's saber fangs dipped and Fargo braced for searing pain, and worse.

THE TRAILSMAN

#370

BLIND MAN'S BLUFF

by

Jon Sharpe

A SIGNET BOOK

SIGNET
Published by New American Library, a division of
Penguin Group (USA) Inc., 375 Hudson Street,
New York, New York 10014, USA
Penguin Group (Canada), 90 Eglinton Avenue East, Suite 700, Toronto,
Ontario M4P 2Y3, Canada (a division of Pearson Penguin Canada Inc.)
Penguin Books Ltd., 80 Strand, London WC2R 0RL, England
Penguin Ireland, 25 St. Stephen's Green, Dublin 2,
Ireland (a division of Penguin Books Ltd.)
Penguin Group (Australia), 250 Camberwell Road, Camberwell, Victoria 3124,
Australia (a division of Pearson Australia Group Pty. Ltd.)
Penguin Books India Pvt. Ltd., 11 Community Centre, Panchsheel Park,
New Delhi - 110 017, India
Penguin Group (NZ), 67 Apollo Drive, Rosedale, Auckland 0632,
New Zealand (a division of Pearson New Zealand Ltd.)
Penguin Books (South Africa) (Pty.) Ltd., 24 Sturdee Avenue,
Rosebank, Johannesburg 2196, South Africa

Penguin Books Ltd., Registered Offices:
80 Strand, London WC2R 0RL, England

First published by Signet, an imprint of New American Library,
a division of Penguin Group (USA) Inc.

First Printing, August 2012
10   9   8   7   6   5   4   3   2   1

The first chapter of this book previously appeared in *Badlands Bloodsport*, the three hundred sixty-ninth volume in this series.

The Trailsman

Beginnings . . . they bend the tree and they mark the man. Skye Fargo was born when he was eighteen. Terror was his midwife, vengeance his first cry. Killing spawned Skye Fargo, ruthless, cold-blooded murder. Out of the acrid smoke of gunpowder still hanging in the air, he rose, cried out a promise never forgotten.

The Trailsman they began to call him all across the West: searcher, scout, hunter, the man who could see where others only looked, his skills for hire but not his soul, the man who lived each day to the fullest, yet trailed each tomorrow. Skye Fargo, the Trailsman, the seeker who could take the wildness of a land and the wanting of a woman and make them his own.

The Chiricahua Mountains, Arizona, 1861—where gold and guns made for a deadly mix.

1

Skye Fargo heard the Apaches before he saw them, which was unusual. Apaches were as silent as wraiths when they wanted to be, and they nearly always wanted to be.

Fargo could move silently, too. A big man, broad of shoulder and narrow at the hips, he wore buckskins, as did most scouts, along with a white hat turned brown from dust and a red bandanna that had seen a lot of use.

He heard yips and instantly drew rein. Some people might mistake them for the yips of coyotes or even the cries of a female fox trying to attract a male, but he knew better.

They were made by human throats.

Fargo was crossing the northern edge of the Chiricahua Mountains. He was to meet in less than a week with an army officer to the east of Apache Pass. So far he'd been able to avoid being spotted by the most feared warriors in all the Southwest.

The yips were repeated. They came from over a rise to Fargo's left. Common sense told him to ride on. But then he heard a cry of pain and he palmed his Colt and rode up the rock-and-boulder-strewn slope to just shy of the crest.

Dismounting, he flattened and crawled the last few yards and poked his head up for a look-see.

There were four of them. Stocky, muscular, bronzed, they wore breechclouts and headbands and the knee-high moccasins for which Apaches were noted. They were Chiricahuas. Only one had a rifle. The others had bows. They were smiling and enjoying themselves, as well they should be, since they were doing what Apaches liked to do just about more than anything: they were torturing an enemy.

In this instance it was a white man. His shabby clothes, the pack mule tied nearby, marked him as a prospector. An ore hound who had been brave enough, or stupid enough, to dare the haunts of the Apache in his search for gold and silver. And they had caught him.

The warrior with the rifle yipped yet again. The rifle, a Sharps, had a rope sling and was slung across his back. In his right hand was a knife with an antler hilt. In his left hand, held in his open palm, were the prospector's eyes; the warrior had just pried them from their sockets.

The prospector wept and groaned and writhed. He was staked out, wrists and ankles. Blood and gore leaked from the dark holes where his eyes had been. He let out a loud sob. "Kill me, you bastard! Kill me now and be done with it."

The warrior who held the eyeballs looked down at him and sneered, "Not yet, white-eye. You suffer much, eh?"

"You son of a bitch, Red Dog," the prospector said.

Fargo focused on the warrior. The name was familiar. Red Dog hated whites with a red-hot hate. Rumor had it his wife had been raped and killed by freighters, and ever since, Red Dog had waged an extermination campaign against anyone with white skin. And since a lot of whites referred to Indians as "red dogs," he'd chosen it as his name in defiance and contempt.

"You know not come our land, Peder-son," Red Dog said.

He stuck the tip of his knife into one of the eyeballs and wagged it under the old prospector's nose. "Want eye back, Peder-son? Here it be. Can you smell it?"

Pederson swore bitterly, then said, "Get it over with, you red wretch. I've never done you or your people any harm."

Red Dog uttered a bark of a laugh. "You white. I red." He dropped to one knee. "You hungry?"

"Eh?" Pederson said. He groaned and coughed. "What do you mean?"

"Have something you can eat," Red Dog said, and poised the eyeball over the unsuspecting prospector's open mouth.

"You wouldn't."

Red Dog laughed.

Fargo had seen enough. He extended the Colt, taking aim at Red Dog's head.

Red Dog bent and lowered the eyeball until it was practically brushing Pederson's lips.

Thumbing back the hammer, Fargo was set to squeeze the trigger when fate played a trump card. One of the other warriors must have caught the glint of sunlight off the Colt because he suddenly pointed and shouted a warning in the Chiricahua tongue.

Just like that, Red Dog exploded into motion. One moment he was hunkered next to the prospector; the next he was up and running, weaving as he ran to make it harder to hit him.

Two other warriors did the same, but the fourth brought up his bow. He already had an arrow nocked and drew the sinew string to his cheek to let fly.

Fargo shot him.

The slug caught the warrior in the sternum and smashed him back. He tottered on his heels, flailed his arms, and crashed down.

The rest had disappeared.

Fargo scoured the terrain. Apaches had an uncanny ability for melting into the earth. He'd witnessed it time and time again. Warily standing, he whistled and the Ovaro came up the slope. He snagged the reins, climbed on, and descended.

In all the commotion the prospector's mule placidly dozed.

"Who's there?" Pederson called out. "God in heaven, be a white man."

"Be still," Fargo cautioned. He rode in a circle, seeking sign of the Apaches. The ground was too rocky to bear tracks. Off a ways, large boulders offered plenty of hiding places.

The skin on his back crawling, Fargo climbed down. He made it a point to hold on to the stallion's reins as he squatted. "Pederson is your handle?"

The old prospector nodded. "Who are you? Did you kill that bastard Red Dog?"

"I killed one, but he and the rest got away," Fargo replied. "Don't move. I'll cut you loose and get you out of here." Dipping his hand into his boot, he palmed the Arkansas toothpick he carried in an ankle sheath.

"I'm obliged," Pederson said, choking with emotion. "I didn't catch your handle."

3

Fargo introduced himself as he cut, keeping one eye on the boulders. He expected Red Dog to try to pick him off with the Sharps.

"That miserable son of a bitch has hankered to get his hands on me for a coon's age," Pederson said. "Always before I had my rifle handy, so he thought twice about it. Today he took me by surprise."

"That's your Sharps he has?"

"It is," Pederson said. "But I forgot to load it after I shot a rabbit last night. He doesn't know that."

"He might by now." Fargo was surprised that the prospector wasn't throwing a fit over his eyes. Most folks would be in hysterics. "How much pain are you in?" he asked.

"Not much at all," Pederson said. "But it's goin' to take some doin' to get used to this dark."

"I'll put bandages on when we're in the clear," Fargo offered.

"My mule, Mabel," Pederson said anxiously. "Did they slit her throat?"

"She's yonder, half-asleep."

"That's my gal," Pederson said. "She doesn't let anything rattle her."

Fargo sliced through the rope on the right wrist and switched to the rope on the left.

"It's my own fault," Pederson said bitterly. "I let down my guard."

"What are you doing in Apache country, anyhow?" Fargo asked, keeping one eye on the boulders. It would only take an instant for an Apache to pop up and let fly with an arrow.

"What else?" Pederson rejoined. "I'm an ore hound, ain't I?"

"But Apache country," Fargo stressed.

"That's just it," Pederson said. "Where better? You must have heard the rumors."

Fargo had. Word was that the Apaches knew of gold and silver veins on their land and guarded the secret with their lives. How else to account for warriors who occasionally showed up at trading posts with pouches of gold or silver, eager to trade for a new rifle or knife or geegaws for their women?

"If a man's careful enough," Pederson was saying, "he can slip in and out of Apache land without them catchin' on."

Fargo stared at the empty sockets where the man's eyes used to be and didn't say anything.

"I know what you're thinkin'," the old prospector said. "But it's worth it."

"It's worth your eyes?"

"To have more money than a body knows what to do with? To live high on the hog?" Pederson nodded and smiled. "What else matters?"

"A sunrise over the prairie," Fargo said. "A high-country lake at sunset."

"What the hell are you? One of them poets?"

"A scout."

"Ah," Pederson said. "A gent who always has to see what's over the next ridge."

"That pretty much pegs me," Fargo admitted, and cut through a loop.

"What pegs me is gold," Pederson said. "More than silver. More than anything." Wincing, he lowered his arms and commenced to rub his wrists. They were raw and bleeding and would need doctoring, too.

Fargo turned to the rope around the left ankle. The Apaches hadn't bothered to strip off the old man's boots, so he could cut without having to worry about hurting the old man.

"Yes, sir," Pederson said. "Red Dog might think he got the better of me. But I'll show him."

"You should take it easy," Fargo suggested.

"Why? Because I lost my eyes? I ain't goin' to let a little thing like that stop me."

Fargo almost said, "You can't prospect blind."

Again, as if he could read Fargo's thoughts, the prospector said, "I'm not licked. I can have others be my eyes for me."

"There aren't many who will come into Apache country," Fargo mentioned.

"It only takes a couple," Pederson said, and chuckled as if at a private joke.

Fargo wondered if maybe the old man's mind had been affected. That would explain how he was taking the loss so calmly.

"Yes, sir," Pederson said. "I know just the pair to help me. I'm already cookin' up a way to have the last laugh on Red Dog."

The reminder made Fargo look up. He'd taken his eyes off the boulders.

Not twenty feet away a swarthy Apache had risen from behind a boulder and was drawing back a bowstring with an arrow nocked to fly.

2

Fargo's reaction was instantaneous. He threw himself to one side. As he dived he dropped the toothpick and swept the Colt clear. He fired as the bowstring twanged. The arrow whizzed past his ear; his slug caught the warrior high on the left side of the chest and spun the Apache half around.

Despite the wound, the warrior grabbed at his quiver for another arrow.

"What's goin' on?" Pederson hollered.

His teeth gritted against the pain, the Chiricahua sought to notch the arrow.

"Drop your bow," Fargo said in the warrior's tongue.

The Apache glanced at him, apparently taken aback that a white man knew his language. He nocked the shaft.

"Is there an Apache?" Pederson said. "Kill him. You hear me? Kill him quick."

"Shut the hell up," Fargo said. He squeezed the trigger as the warrior was about to let fly. This time he aimed at the Chiricahua's head. He didn't miss.

Pederson must have heard the body fall because he chortled with glee. "You did it! But if you ask me, you're too damn slow to kill. Why'd you warn him to drop his bow?"

"I don't kill unless I have to."

"Well, that's stupid."

Keeping the Colt in his right hand, Fargo picked up the Arkansas toothpick and turned to the last rope.

"I've seen turtles that were faster at cuttin' than you are."

"Keep it up." Fargo slashed, once, twice, and the job was done. Sliding the toothpick into its ankle sheath, he stood. "On your feet. We need to light a shuck."

"Aren't you goin' to help me up?"

7

"I'm slow, remember?"

"Touchy, too. Give me a minute." Pederson struggled to rise and slowly sat up. "I can't hardly feel my hands and my feet."

Fargo watched the boulders. The Apaches would want revenge for the two he'd killed.

Pederson rubbed his legs while turning his head from side to side. "God," he said. "This'll take some gettin' used to."

"You're taking it better than most would," Fargo mentioned.

The old man shrugged. "I never have let things bother me much. That time I chopped off my little toe by accident when I was eleven or so—"

"By accident?" Fargo said.

"I was choppin' wood for my ma and I got careless and missed the log." Pederson grinned. "I cut through my boot and the toe oozed out the hole with the blood. It would have been comical if it hadn't hurt so much. I picked up the toe and took it in to show her."

"Bet she loved that."

"You should have heard her squeal," Pederson said, and chortled.

"You lost a lot more than a toe this time," Fargo remarked, but the prospector didn't seem to hear him.

"Then there was the time an ornery mustang about stove in my back. This was before I got Mabel. I was tryin' to break the horse. It threw me and stomped me into the dirt. I was up and about inside of a month."

"You're one tough buzzard."

"It's not that so much as I do what needs doin'."

Fargo thought he heard a pebble rattle and spun but saw only boulders. "Hurry up."

"Worried about an arrow in the back, are you?" Pederson said. He stopped rubbing, put his hands flat on the ground, and attempted to stand. "Damn these feet of mine, anyhow."

Quickly, Fargo bent and hoisted him up. For a few moments Pederson swayed, then steadied.

"Lead me to Mabel, if you'd be so kind."

"We'll have to leave your supplies," Fargo said. The mule

was laden with packs and tools, including a shovel and a pick.

"Like hell we will," Pederson said. "I can't prospect without them."

"You can't ride her with all those packs tied on."

"Who said anything about ridin'?" Pederson rejoined. "I was fixin' to lead her like I usually do."

"When you can't see?"

"You can guide me."

"It would slow us down too much," Fargo said. And give the Apaches that much more of an opportunity to pick them off.

"I'm not ditchin' my grub and whatnot and that's final," Pederson insisted.

Fargo swore. "You can ride double with me, then." He pulled the oldster around to the side of the Ovaro and placed Pederson's hand on the saddle. "Can you climb up on your own?"

"I'm blind," Pederson said. "I ain't helpless."

It took him three tries, but he got on and slid back to make room.

Careful to watch the boulders, Fargo hooked his boot in the stirrup and swung his other leg up and over. He expected arrows to streak at him, but none did. Anxious to get out of there, he brought the Ovaro alongside Mabel. He snagged the mule's lead rope, shoved it into the prospector's hand, and said, "Hold on to this. And hang on yourself."

"I know how to ride, you simpleton."

They started out at a walk, Fargo twisting to watch behind them.

Pederson suddenly threw back his head and hollered, "You hear me, Red Dog? This ain't over. I'll be back, and I'll make you pay."

The silence mocked them.

"He heard me, all right," Pederson told Fargo. "He's too high and mighty to answer, though."

A small object came flying out of nowhere and struck the old man on the shoulder. It bounced off and fell to the dirt with a plop.

"What was that?" Pederson asked, unruffled.

Fargo looked down. He was used to the brutal violence of the frontier, but his gut churned and he tasted bile.

"One of your eyes." It lay on the stem, the pupil fixed on the stallion. He tapped his spurs.

"Really? Turn around and fetch it for me."

"What the hell for?"

"As a keepsake."

Fargo kept on riding.

"Didn't you hear me?"

"My ears work, you simpleton."

"Oh." Pederson chuckled. "You give as good as you get, don't you, sonny?"

"Sometimes worse," Fargo said.

Fargo didn't breathe easy until they had covered about a quarter of a mile. He deemed it unlikely the Apaches would come after them on foot.

"I would have fetched my eye if you'd let me," Pederson said sullenly.

"No more about the damn eye."

"Oh, sure. It wasn't yours. What do you care?"

Pederson muttered something, then said, "You can be grumpy—you know that? I'm the one who had his eyes poked out and I'm in a better mood than you are."

"The last thing you want to do," Fargo said, "is prod me."

"Ah. I savvy now," Pederson said. "You're one of those hard cases."

Fargo had been told that on more than one occasion, so he figured it must be true, but all he said was "If you say so."

"If we can't talk eyes, can I ask where you're takin' me?"

"I haven't thought that far ahead," Fargo said. "I'm headed southeast to meet with a Major Coult near Apache Pass." The army planned to build a fort in the region and wanted his help in finding the best spot.

"Southeast?" Pederson said. "Then how about you take me to Cemetery?"

"Where?"

"Cemetery," Pederson repeated. "It's a settlement about halfway between here and the Pass."

Fargo had never heard of it, and said so.

"It sprung up about, oh, seven or eight months ago,"

Pederson revealed. "They've got a trading post and a saloon and not much else."

"The saloon is enough," Fargo said. "But a settlement in the middle of Apache country?"

"It won't be Apache country forever," Pederson said. "The man who owns the post thinks it won't be long before folks come pourin' in. Land is cheap and there's plenty for everyone."

"The Apaches might have something to say about that."

"Enough whites move in, we'll lick 'em good and proper."

Fargo had a hunch the new settlement had something to do with the army's decision to build a new fort. "How many people live there already?"

"In Cemetery? I ain't ever counted 'em, but I'd reckon six or seven."

"That's all?" Fargo was surprised they hadn't been wiped out, and said so.

"To tell the truth, I'm a mite surprised myself. McKindrick, the man who runs the trading post, ain't much of a fightin' man. He can wrestle a pie or a cake, but he'd be helpless against an Apache."

"Not many can hold their own against them."

"I'd say there are a lot of whites who can, but my eyeballs make a liar out of me."

After that the old man was quiet.

Arizona in the summer was no place for amateurs. The burning sun made a furnace of the air and baked the land like an oven. By noon the temperature was well above a hundred. Signs of life were few: a solitary hawk wheeling high in the sky, a lizard that skittered from their path, a glossy snake sunning itself.

Dust rose with every clomp of the Ovaro's hoofs. The same with Mabel, who plodded along with the tireless stamina of her kind.

Fargo pulled his hat brim low against the glare. He was thirsty, but they had a ways to go and his canteen was only half-full.

"Tell me something, sonny." Pederson broke his silence. "How bad do I look?"

Fargo replied without turning his head, "Bad."

"So I shouldn't walk around like I am? It might turn peoples' stomachs?"

"It damned near turned mine."

Pederson sighed. "When we get to Cemetery, the first thing I'd better do is rig somethin' to tie over the holes."

Fargo drew rein.

"What are you doin'?" Pederson asked.

Not answering, Fargo shifted and reached past the prospector and opened his saddlebag. He rummaged a bit and found his spare bandanna. Folding it in half and then in half again, he pressed it to the old man's eyes.

Pederson gave a start. "What are you—" He stopped. "Oh. It's awful decent of you."

"Don't tell anyone," Fargo said.

"I'm obliged." Pederson stiffened and cocked his head.

"Hold still." Fargo was trying to knot it behind the man's head.

"Didn't you hear that?" Pederson asked.

"Hear what?"

"I think we're bein' followed."

3

Fargo tied the knot and listened intently. His hearing was better than most and he didn't hear anything to cause alarm. After another minute he said, "You're imagining things."

"I tell you I heard footsteps," Pederson insisted. "Red Dog must be following us."

It was possible, Fargo supposed. Apaches were incredibly hardy. They could cover up to seventy-five miles at a time at a steady jog. "We'll find out."

He gigged the Ovaro. In a while the land started to climb. Enormous boulders reared, some bigger than a cabin, and the next he came to, he reined around to the other side and stopped.

Shucking his Henry from the saddle scabbard, Fargo dismounted. "You can stay up there or you can climb down and sit. We're liable to be here awhile."

"You're fixin' to wait and surprise 'em," Pederson guessed, and grinned. "Put one between Red Dog's eyes for me." He awkwardly climbed down, then groped along the boulder.

"That spot is good," Fargo suggested. "You're in the shade."

"I can feel it."

Fargo had heard that blind people developed sharper senses, but Pederson had only been blind a short while. "Do you want water?"

"No need," the prospector said. "I can go days without." Sinking down with his back to the boulder, he put his hands to the bandanna. "This feels strange. Maybe when we get to Cemetery I'll fix myself up with a couple of patches."

"Why did they name the settlement that?" Fargo had been meaning to ask.

"It was McKindrick's doin'," Pederson said. "Folks told him he was loco to open a trading post in Apache country. They said he might as well dig his own grave in the cemetery. To prove them wrong, that's what he named it." Pederson chuckled. "People do silly stuff, don't they?"

Fargo was amazed at the good mood the old man was in. If it were him, he'd be miserable. "Be quiet now," he advised, and moved around to where he could see their back trail. Flattening in shadow so the gleam of the sun wouldn't reflect off his Henry, he settled in to wait.

The withering heat made it hard to concentrate. Fargo was constantly wiping sweat from his brow with his sleeve. If it got into his eyes they'd sting and blur, and he needed his vision clear.

He gave it half an hour. Other than a fly doing its best to annoy him, the blistered landscape was barren of life.

Rising, Fargo returned to the Ovaro and shoved the Henry into the scabbard.

Pederson had been dozing. Now he snorted and sat up.

"Nothin'?"

"Not a sign."

"I was so sure." Pederson tiredly rubbed his stubble. "Maybe my mind is playin' tricks on me. I'm feelin' a little puny."

"You're holding up better than most would."

"Grubbin' for gold all these years trimmed the fat off of me. Body and mind."

"Let's get you up."

Soon they were under way. After a while the old prospector slumped in the saddle and showed other signs that his ordeal was finally catching up to him.

Fargo stopped early for the night in a cluster of boulders atop a hill. The only way to get at them was through a gap barely wide enough for the Ovaro. He stripped the saddle and spread out his bedroll and had Pederson lie down.

"What about you? What will you use?"

"I'll be keeping watch," Fargo said.

"That's not fair. I should take a turn so that you can—" Pederson stopped. "Listen to me. I'm bein' plumb stupid."

"It will take some getting used to."

"I don't know as I can," Pederson said bitterly. "It galls a man to be less than he used to be."

Fargo would have liked to make coffee to help him stay awake, but they were too short on water. He sat cross-legged near the gap, the Henry across his lap.

The gray of twilight gave way to the indigo of descending night. Stars sparkled in the firmament like a legion of fireflies. Somewhere a coyote yowled a lonely lament.

The heat dissipated, and for that Fargo was grateful.

He smothered a yawn and passed the time thinking about ladies he'd known. There were a lot. He could have kept at it every night for a week and not gone through them all. As it was, along about the middle of the night the Ovaro raised its head and nickered and he was instantly alert.

Something was out there.

Fargo sensed it rather than heard it. When it growled he raised the Henry to his shoulder. It didn't sound like a coyote, and coyotes seldom stalked people, anyway. It could be a wolf, he reckoned, but they were rare that far south. He suspected a big cat. Maybe a mountain lion that had picked up the stallion's scent.

The growl was repeated. It was so low and so deep, Fargo wondered if it was a jaguar. They were rare, too, and far more dangerous than any wolf.

As still as a statue, Fargo waited. His shoulder began to ache, but he held the Henry steady. He mustn't miss with his first shot. A wounded jaguar was savagery incarnate.

Pederson was snoring. Not loudly, but enough that it would drown out the stealthy pad of feline paws.

Twenty minutes must have passed when Fargo finally lowered the rifle. He figured the cat had moved on. When the Ovaro nickered again he glanced over and saw that the stallion was staring up at the sky.

No, not the sky, Fargo realized with a start. The Ovaro was staring at the top of a boulder, at a spot he couldn't see. Heaving to his feet, Fargo backpedaled.

As he came out of the dark shadow, he spied a large form crouched twenty feet up.

Even as he saw it, the jaguar snarled.

Fargo fired, worked the lever, and went to fire again, but the cat sprang. Darting aside, he fired as the jaguar alighted, fired as it spun toward him.

The jaguar leaped.

A flashing paw tipped with razor claws swiped at Fargo's throat. He barely got the Henry up in time to block. The force made him stagger. Regaining his balance, he went to fire.

"What's goin' on?" Pederson hollered.

Crouching, the jaguar hissed at the old man and then came at Fargo in a rush. A forepaw caught the Henry's muzzle and a claw must have hooked the sight because the next moment the rifle was torn from Fargo's grasp.

Fargo stabbed for his Colt. He was clearing leather when the jaguar slammed into him like a fur-clad avalanche. The impact bowled him over and he wound up on his back with the big cat astride his chest. Glistening fangs were poised over his face. He tried to draw, but his arm was pinned. The cat's saber fangs dipped and Fargo braced for searing pain, and worse. But instead of biting him, the jaguar's chin came to rest on his chest and the cat collapsed.

"Fargo?" Pederson bawled. "Are you all right? What's goin' on?"

Fargo blinked. The jaguar was just lying there. Its eyes were locked on his and its mouth was spread wide, but it didn't move or make a sound. He touched its side with his free hand and nothing happened. "I'll be damned," he said, and exhaled.

"What?" Pederson said. He had sat up and was twisting right and left. "Where are you? Was that a mountain lion? Where did it go?"

"It's right here," Fargo said. By pushing and wriggling he managed to extricate himself. He'd been lucky, damned lucky. One of his shots had finally taken effect. He looked down at himself and couldn't believe he wasn't so much as scratched. His relief was so potent, he laughed.

"What's so funny?" Pederson said. "Talk to me, damn it."

Fargo enlightened him. "It was a jaguar. It's dead."

"A jag?" Pederson got to his hands and knees and slowly rose. His hands out in front of him, he shuffled over. "Where? Let me touch it."

"Another couple of steps and you'll trip over the thing," Fargo warned. He reclaimed the Henry and fed a cartridge into the chamber.

Kneeling, Pederson roved his hands over the powerfully body. "My God," he said. "This is a big 'un."

That it was. A male, it was close to seven feet long from the tip of its nose to the end of its tail. Its weight Fargo pegged at between two hundred and fifty and three hundred pounds.

"We have to skin it," Pederson said.

"Why bother?" Fargo responded. The skinning would take most of the night.

"Don't you know how much a jag hide can fetch? Why, it'd buy me enough grub to last me pretty near a year. We can tote the hide out on Mabel and—" Pederson caught himself, and frowned. "I'm doin' it again, ain't I?"

"You are," Fargo said.

"I'm actin' like I'm normal when I ain't," Pederson said. "And I won't be ever again."

Fargo stared at the dead cat, thinking. "It would give you some money to get by for a while."

"I don't need charity," Pederson said. "If you skin it, we split fifty-fifty."

Fargo changed his mind. He'd peel the hide, after all. Leaning the Henry against a boulder, he drew his Arkansas toothpick. It wasn't as big as a bowie or most skinning knives, but it would do. Hunkering, he set to work.

First he cut the large tendon that ran down the right rear leg where the tendon met the heel. Hooking his finger into the hole, he proceeded to pull and tug and wrest with the gradually loosening hide. If done right, it came off in one piece. Some hunters used a knife to peel the hide away and inevitably nicked and cut it, reducing its value. He used only his hands.

"I can help," Pederson offered. "I've skinned more than a few cats in my day."

"Why not?" Fargo said. He positioned him and guided his hands to the hide, and Pederson went at it in earnest.

Fargo turned to the other rear leg.

Working together, they rolled the hide up over the jaguar's haunches. They'd peeled it midway up the body when Pederson paused to catch his breath.

"This takes some doin', and I ain't as young as I used to be." The old prospector patted the cat's head. "A Pima once told me that jaguars usually hunt in pairs. I wonder if it's true."

Fargo was about to say he doubted it when he happened to glance at the gap into their sanctuary.

Another jaguar was crouched in the opening.

4

"Look out!" Fargo cried, and clawed for his Colt. His hand was so slick with blood and gore that as he drew, the revolver slipped free and clattered noisily to the ground at his feet. He scooped it up with both hands and turned toward the opening, only to find the other jaguar wasn't there. Wiping his right hand on his buckskins, he gripped the Colt securely. A few strides brought him to the gap. Poking his head out, he surveyed the stark landscape. "It's gone."

"What is?" Pederson asked. He had frozen in the act of peeling more hide.

"There was another jaguar."

"I didn't know what to do," Pederson said. "You didn't say what it was."

On hindsight, Fargo reflected that yelling "Look out!" to a blind man was about as stupid as could be. Holstering the Colt, he came back. "Let's finish and I'll stand watch until daybreak."

Once the pelt was off, Fargo used a rock to crack open the jaguar's skull. He dipped his hand in, scooped out the brains, and rubbed them over the inside of the hide. Finally he spread the hide out, hair down, to dry.

"I'm obliged for all the trouble you're goin' to on my account," Pederson remarked.

"What will you do once we reach Cemetery?" Fargo asked. "Do you have a wife somewhere?"

"Had one," Pederson said. "The best gal who ever drew breath. About five years ago, it was, she took sick with the croup and died."

"Other kin?" Fargo said. "Brothers or sisters or cousins who will take you in?"

Pederson snorted. "Hell, I haven't see any of them in a coon's age. Last I heard, one of my brothers went off to South America or some such place and that was the last we heard from him. My sis is married to a deacon who thinks I'm the worst sinner this side of Judas."

"Anyone else?"

"I've got a younger brother who has two kids. They might be willin' to lend a hand. They wrote to me a couple of years ago, but I never got around to answerin'."

The prospector didn't elaborate and Fargo didn't pry. The rest of the night was uneventful and at first light they were under way, the jaguar hide rolled up and tied on Mabel.

It was the middle of the morning on the fourth day when Fargo crested a ridge and saw several buildings in the heat haze a mile off.

"That would be Cemetery," Pederson said on hearing the news.

The old man had fallen into a funk the day after the jaguar attack and had been moody and mostly silent since.

Several times Fargo tried to make small talk, but he might as well have tried to talk to a tree. Suddenly that changed.

"You won't leave me right away, will you?"

"Hadn't planned on it," Fargo said. "I can spare another day before I have to head out to meet the major."

"I'm obliged," Pederson said. "I'd like to get me a room at the boardin'house."

"Next you'll be telling me there's a hotel," Fargo said.

Pederson grinned. "McKindrick's wife lets a few spare rooms at the back of their place, is all."

Fargo wasn't expecting much, and he wasn't disappointed.

Cemetery lived up to its name. A dog lay in the shade of the trading post, a plank affair that looked fit to tumble down at the first strong wind. The saloon had a front doorway but no batwings or door and a front window but no glass. There was one house. It had a picket fence, of all things, and grass as brown as dirt. A flower garden, without any flowers, bordered a small porch. Several horses were at the hitch rails, half dozing and lazily swishing their tails.

Pederson asked Fargo to take him to the house. A sign nailed to a porch post read ROOMS FOR RENT. Fargo knocked and stepped back so the prospector could do the talking. He had no interest whatsoever in anything having to do with Cemetery. Or so he thought.

Then the front door opened.

She wasn't much over thirty. Golden hair fell in cascading curls to just above her emerald eyes. Ruby lips added to her allure. Her fashionable dress was prim enough but couldn't hide her more than ample bosom or how her legs seemed to go forever. Shocked, she put a hand to her creamy throat and exclaimed, "Mr. Pederson? Is that you?"

"Afraid so, ma'am," the prospector said. "I must look a sight and for that I'm sorry."

The vision clasped one of his hands in concern. "What on earth happened?"

Pederson tried to answer but became too choked up to speak. Coughing, he bowed his head and shook it.

Fargo stepped out of the shadows. "Apaches, ma'am," he said. "They cut out his eyes."

Those emerald eyes of hers focused on him with more than mild interest. "Oh my. I didn't see you there. Who might you be?"

Pederson said, "This is Fargo, ma'am. He scouts for the army. He saved me when those red devils were about to do me in." Pederson gestured at her. "Fargo, this is Mrs. McKindrick. Mary is her first name."

"How do you do?" Mary said, holding out her hand for him to shake.

Fargo let his gaze drift from her hair to her polished shoes to the swell of her hips. "You're married to the gent who runs the trading post?"

"I'm his common-law wife," Mary McKindrick said. She added with a hint of resentment, "I doubt he'll ever stand before a minister and say 'I do.'"

"Is he loco?" Fargo asked with a grin.

Mary smiled, caught herself, and said to Pederson, "What can I do for you, Abner?"

It was the first Fargo had heard the prospector's first name.

"I was hopin' you might have one of your rooms to let," Pederson said. "I need a place to rest up for a spell."

"Say no more," Mary McKindrick said. "I happen to have a couple of rooms free at the moment, and one is yours for as long as you'd like to stay." She paused. "Provided Abe doesn't mind, you understand?"

"I doubt he would," Pederson said. "Him and me get along right fine."

"Well, you know how he is," Mary said. "You can pay for the room, can't you?"

"Those devils took my eyeballs but not my poke," Pederson said. "I reckon I've got me a couple of months' worth of rent money."

"Good." Mary pumped his hand enthusiastically, and turned to Fargo. "And you, sir? Do you require a room as well?"

Fargo hadn't intended to stay more than a few hours and be on his way. But he could leave bright and early in the morning and still meet up with Major Coult on time. "Why not?"

"I serve supper at seven, breakfast at six," Mary recited. "We ask that there be no loud noises after ten, and no carrying on whatsoever with liquor and whatnot."

"I'm fond of whatnot," Fargo said, and winked.

Mary blushed. "Be that as it may, there will be none of that on these premises. My husband is very strict about such things."

"My condolences, ma'am," Fargo said.

Mary laughed, and once again caught herself. "You are a handful, sir."

"A lot of ladies have told me that."

"Have they, now?"

Pederson coughed. "If you two are done teasin' each other, I'd like to rest up awhile."

"Oh. Abner. I'm sorry. I'll take you to your room." Mary guided him inside and said to Fargo, "I'll show you yours as well."

Fargo lowered his hand to near his crotch, and pointed. "It's right here."

Where some women might have been offended, Mary McKindrick chuckled. "More than a handful, I bet."

"Have you ever been to the redwoods out in California?" Fargo asked.

Mary looked him in the eye. "No. I've always wanted to see a redwood, though."

Pederson said, "What's all this nonsense about trees? I really would like to lie down for a bit."

"Of course. Come along."

The rooms were on the ground floor at the back of the house, past the kitchen. An addition had been built for that purpose, Mary explained as she ushered Abner into the first empty one. It was small and spare; there was a bed and a washbasin and a chamber pot, and that was it.

"What, no chandelier?" Fargo said from the doorway.

Mary grinned. "This isn't a fancy hotel. And my husband didn't see any sense in squandering money on refinements for boarders. It's not as if we get all that many."

"Mr. McKindrick is tight with his money, is he?" Fargo asked.

"Mr. McKindrick is tight with a lot of things," Mary said. She drew Pederson over to his bed and he gratefully sank onto his side with his head on the pillow.

"If you could wake me in an hour, ma'am, I'd be grateful. All I need is a little nap. I'll fetch my things later."

"You can pay me then, too," Mary said. "My husband always wants the money up front."

"Of course he does," Fargo said.

Mary colored again, but for a different reason, and quietly closed the door. "Come along. I'll show you to yours."

It was the next room down, and it was exactly like the first.

Fargo deliberately stood so close to her that they practically brushed bodies. He swore he could feel heat come off her in waves. Sniffing, he remarked, "That's nice perfume you wear."

"No one hardly ever notices," Mary said rather huskily.

"Like I said, your husband must be loco."

"That'll be enough about him." Marcy held out her hand. "A dollar, if you please."

Fargo fished out a coin and set it in her palm. As he drew back his hand, he lightly caressed hers with the tip of his finger. "There you go."

"Thank you," Mary said, and turned. "I have to see about putting supper on. It promises to be a busy night."

"How are the stars here?" Fargo asked.

"The stars?" Mary repeated. "I'm sure I don't know. Why?"

"Ever want to go for a walk in the starlight?" Fargo said, and winked.

Mary McKindrick folded her arms across her chest. "You, sir, are one of *those*."

"I sure am, ma'am," Fargo said.

5

Claiming she had duties to attend to, Mary McKindrick bustled off.

Fargo had duties of his own. He led the Ovaro and Mabel around to the back of the house. Instead of a corral the McKindricks had a long shed open on one side, with stalls for animals. He stripped his saddle and saddlebags from the Ovaro and the packs from Mabel and placed them in adjoining stalls. There was a trough for water and a bin with oats.

The sun was well on its downward slant when Fargo decided to see what Cemetery had to offer by way of entertainment. First he went to the trading post. It had the usual trade goods and tools and several rifles and guns. He was examining a Remington in a case when a heavyset man with no hair to speak of and a porcine face came over.

"Can I help you, sir?"

"You must be Abe McKindrick," Fargo said. An easy deduction since there wasn't anyone else in the place.

"In the flesh," McKindrick said, and gestured proudly. "This is my establishment."

"The boardinghouse, too, I've been told," Fargo said. "You're a man of many means."

"You've been over to the house?" McKindrick asked with a hint of suspicion.

"I took a room," Fargo revealed to see how the trader would react, and was secretly amused at the fleeting anger that lit his porkish eyes. Then, to set McKindrick at ease, he told about finding Abner Pederson, and the condition the prospector was in.

"That poor man," McKindrick said, without a shred of

sympathy. "But then, he knew the risk he took, going out alone in Apache country." He paused. "You say he intends to rent a room for a spell?"

"His exact words."

"I wonder if he has the money to pay for it."

Fargo hid his disgust. "He said he did. I think he plans to send for some kin for help."

"Ah." McKindrick smiled. "Well, he's welcome to stay for as long as he likes. Never let it be said I refused to help someone in need." He paused again. "How about you? How long are you staying?"

"I have to head out at first light."

"That's too bad," McKindrick said, making it sound as if it were the best news in all creation.

Fargo needed a drink.

The saloon wasn't half the size of the trading post. It boasted two tables and a long board set on barrels that served as the bar. The bartender was playing solitaire and chewing on a toothpick.

"Lively place," Fargo said.

"It'll pick up along about sundown," the barkeep said without looking up. "By midnight I'll have six or seven customers."

"You beat St. Louis saloons all hollow," Fargo said.

The man grinned. "Ain't you funny? What can I fix you with?"

"Coffin varnish," Fargo said. "Hold the ice."

The bartender laughed and selected a bottle of Monongahela from a shelf. He took a dirty glass and filled it two-thirds full and set it on the bar. "That'll be two bits."

"Is that so?" Fargo said, and took the bottle instead. Tilting it, he swallowed a few times, let out an "Ahhhh," and wiped his mouth with his sleeve.

"You didn't say you wanted the bottle."

"You didn't ask." Fargo treated himself to another swig and held it out. "Care for one on me?"

The barman brightened. "Mister, we are best friends forever." He happily chugged and burped and gave the bottle back. "Most hereabouts are too selfish to share."

"Would you be talking about Abe McKindrick?"

Snorting, the barman said, "Mr. High and Mighty? Set foot in here? Are you joshing?"

"I don't know the man that well."

"Let's put it this way," the bartender said. "He's God's gift to creation and proud of it."

"Somebody up there must like him," Fargo said, "the wife he's got."

"Oh. Her." The barman glanced at the doorless doorway and lowered his voice. "Between you and me, I don't see what she sees in him. I mean, I hear tell he hardly ever touches her. Can you imagine? A fine figure of a female like that?"

"I know I'd touch her."

The barman guffawed. "Makes two of us. But they're man and wife, so she's off the market."

"I hear she doesn't wear a ring."

Shrugging, the barkeep said, "She still considers herself hitched."

Fargo regarded the empty chairs and the dusty walls and a spittoon that hadn't been cleaned since Adam and Eve, and said, "I have to ask. Why in hell did you pick here, of all places?"

"I got into a little trouble back East," the man said. "I worked a bar back there and one night a drunk came at me with a knife."

"Self-defense," Fargo said.

"Except that when I squeezed the trigger, he'd turned his back to me." The barman frowned. "And his cousin was the county sheriff."

"Damn," Fargo said.

"So I drifted. I had a little saved. Enough that I was looking to start a place of my own."

"But *here*?"

"I figure that sheriff won't come this far. I'll stay a year or so and if things don't pick up, I hear California is the place to be."

"To California," Fargo said. He drank and passed the bottle over.

"To Mrs. McKindrick," the barman proposed, and drank.

He gnawed his lip a bit, then said, "This is just for you being so neighborly, you understand."

"What is?"

"Abe McKindrick works late most nights."

"How late?"

"Some nights he doesn't blow out the wick and go home until past ten." The barman gazed out the glassless window at the trading post. "Probably fondling his money when he should be fondling her."

"Do tell," Fargo said.

"If I was as young as you and as good-looking as you, it'd be something to know."

"The rest of the bottle is yours," Fargo said. He paid and left and strolled around to the rear of the boardinghouse.

Parched land stretched for as far as the eye could see. Other than the mountains in the distance, the only break in the monotony was the road to the east, if it could be called that. Pockmarked by hooves and lined by the ruts of wagon wheels, it disappeared into the haze.

"Pretty dismal, isn't it?" said a sultry voice behind him.

Fargo turned. "What do you do for fun around here? Stomp grasshoppers?"

Mary McKindrick laughed a hollow laugh. "Fun? What's that? I can't remember the last time I had fun."

"You're overdue," Fargo said.

Mary continued to stare off into the distance. "We don't always have a choice, do we?"

"Are we still talking about fun?"

"No," Mary said. She studied him. "I was watching you out the front window." She quickly mentioned, "I usually sit in my rocker and knit and look out the window."

"That's not fun?"

"You're not half as clever as you think you are," Mary said lightheartedly. But she promptly sobered. "Why did you go over to the trading post?"

"It's the only one in town."

"Be serious for a minute. I noticed you didn't buy anything."

"I was taking a measure," Fargo said.

"Of the post?"

"No."

"Oh." Her cheeks grew pink. She pinched her lips and dug at the ground with a toe and said, "You have to understand."

"It's none of my affair," Fargo said.

"I was married once. He was nice enough for a while and then he took to drinking and beating me. It got so, one night he broke my arm."

"You don't have to tell me this."

Mary went on anyway. "I left him. Up and ran off. I couldn't afford an attorney and never did get a divorce. And not many men will take up with a married woman unless it's for one thing and one thing only."

"And then along came McKindrick."

Mary nodded. "He thinks I'm pretty and he'd never, ever hit me. So I figured, why not?"

"He's safe," Fargo said. "But a lot like the view." He motioned at the bleak terrain that went on forever.

"Damn you," Mary said softly.

"No one is twisting your arm," Fargo said. "You do or you don't—it's up to you."

"Damn you, damn you, damn you." She turned and made for the back door but stopped and looked at him almost pleadingly. "I don't mean that."

"I know."

"You'll stay the night, then?"

"I already paid for the room."

Mary fluffed at her hair and said, "I must be a terrible person to have the thoughts I've been having."

"Everyone should have some fun now and then," Fargo said.

"Is that all you think of?"

"It's up there with whiskey and cards," Fargo confessed.

"I should be offended, but I'm not. Truth is, I'm kind of flattered." She hesitated. "You're not one of those braggarts, are you?"

Fargo held his hands about two feet apart. "I cannot tell a lie," he said. "It's this big."

Mary burst out in a laugh that brought her to tears. When

she had collected herself, she dabbed at her eyes and said, "You, sir, are naughty as sin. But thank you. I needed that. I also need an answer. I don't want to be tossed out on my ear. When I go, I want it to be my doing."

"From your thighs to my mouth and no further," Fargo said.

Mary laughed some more. "Goodness, I like you. I believe you, too." She sashayed to the door and opened it and looked at him. "Thank you," she said softly.

"Just remember I warned you," Fargo said, and held his hands wide apart.

The door closed and her mirth tinkled gaily.

"One of us," Fargo said to the Ovaro, "just might get lucky tonight."

6

Candles cast a golden glow over the china plates and the silverware. Glasses of water had been set out, along with a butter dish and a sugar bowl.

Fargo was the last to take his seat. He'd gone to his room to wash up and trim his beard. He'd also taken his spare buckskin shirt from his saddlebags and cleaned his boots. Now, scrubbed and smelling of lye soap, he sank down across from Abner Pederson.

The old man had also done some washing and scrubbing. He'd even washed the bandanna that covered his eyes.

At the near end of the table sat Mary McKindrick. At the far end, her husband.

Another boarder, a drummer by the name of Waxman, was chattering about women's corsets.

"You're just in time, Mr. Fargo," Mary broke in, sounding grateful for the interruption. "Another minute and we would have started without you."

"Yes," Abe McKindrick said. "Kindly be punctual at mealtime. It's not polite to keep everyone waiting."

"I was having fun," Fargo said.

Mary covered her mouth with her hand, her eyes twinkling.

"Fun, sir?" Abe McKindrick repeated. "Grown men don't have fun. They're too busy earning a living."

"Not me," Fargo said. "If I don't have fun at least once a week, I get as mean as a riled bear."

"What a strange thing for a scout to say," Abe McKindrick said. "The last time I had fun was when I was ten years old."

"I believe it," Fargo said.

"You should. In addition to my other virtues, I'm a man of my word."

"How many virtues do you have, exactly?" Fargo asked.

"I have two."

"That's all?"

Mary cleared her throat. "Perhaps we should start to eat? I don't want the food to grow cold."

"Certainly, my dear," McKindrick said.

The meal consisted of beef stew with carrots and chopped string beans, freshly baked bread, and a pudding speckled with raisins.

Fargo was famished. He smeared butter on a thick slice of bread, dipped it in the stew, and closed his eyes. "My compliments to the cook."

"Mary does wonderfully, doesn't she?" McKindrik said. "Her cooking is what persuaded me to take her into my house."

"They say the way to a man's heart is through his stomach," Mary said with a cold smile.

"That it is, my dear," McKindrik said while forking a piece of beef. "Wouldn't you agree, Mr. Fargo?"

"There are things I like more than food," Fargo said.

"What, for instance?"

"Fun."

"You keep bringing that up," McKindrik said. "A body would think it's all you have on your mind."

Fargo glanced at Mary. "It is."

Abner Pederson broke his silence with "What I'd like to know is when the next stage comes through."

"Stage?" McKindrick said, his mouth crammed with stew. "I'm afraid we're not on any stage line yet."

"But I have mail to get out."

"A mud wagon stops every couple of weeks or so," McKindrik said. He stopped chewing and scratched his chin. "You might be in luck. I believe it's due in the next couple of days."

Fargo was admiring Mary out of the corner of his eye. Was it his imagination or was there a gloss to her lips that hadn't been there before? And a touch of rouge on her cheeks? He liked how her bosom swelled when she reached for the butter, and the rustle of her dress. Suddenly he realized her husband was talking to him.

"—assessment of the situation. As a scout you must have insights on how to deal with them."

"Which situation is that?" Fargo asked.

"Why, the Apaches, of course. Abner here was just saying how he lost his eyes to that vile butcher, the one they call Red Dog."

"That's hardly proper dinner conversation," Mary chided.

McKindrick shot her an irritated look. "Be that as it may, the Apaches are a real and constant threat. I'd like Mr. Fargo's opinion."

Fargo wasn't sure what the trader was getting at. So he said simply, "Leave."

"I beg your pardon?"

"Leave," Fargo said again. "Pack up and go. Or sooner or later Red Dog will get around to paying you a visit."

"He won't attack us," McKindrick said smugly.

"What's to stop him? There's not ten of you in the whole settlement. He could wipe you out without half trying."

"Red Dog isn't stupid. He knows it would bring the army down on his head."

"The army goes after him, he'll have them chasing their own tails."

"It almost sounds, sir," McKindrick said, "as if you're singing his praises."

"I'm making a point," Fargo said. "Red Dog is no more afraid of the army than he is of a toad."

"You're not suggesting our cavalrymen are too timid, by any chance?"

"Quit putting words in my mouth. I'm saying that if Red Dog decides to burn Cemetery to the ground, you have a snowball's chance in hell of stopping him."

"We're not leaving," McKindrick said. "I'd be a fool to pack up and go after all the work and expense I've gone to. Besides, in ten years Cemetery will have grown into a town and then the Apaches won't dare give us trouble."

Fargo turned to Mary. "How about you? Do you feel safe here?"

"My feelings don't enter into it," she said. "I go where he goes and do what he wants me to do."

"Must be fun," Fargo said.

The drummer coughed and opened his mouth as if to say something but didn't.

That was the end of small talk for a while.

Fargo noticed that the others kept looking at Pederson. The prospector was bent over his bowl and using his spoon carefully so as not to spill any stew.

It was Abe McKindrick who eventually said, "So, tell me, Abner. These relatives you're sending for. What are your plans?"

"I've been thinkin' about what to do for days now," Pederson said. "It galls me, Red Dog gougin' out my eyes and I can't make him pay."

"What can you do to him, blind as you are?"

Pederson frowned. "That's what is takin' some gettin' used to."

"I wasn't talking about revenge," McKindrick said. "I meant what will you do for a living?"

"I've been thinkin' about that, too. I sure don't aim to go around helpless the rest of my days. I ain't ever depended on folks and I ain't about to start now."

"Still, what can you do?"

Pederson sat back and seemed to be wrestling with himself and finally he said, "I reckon the thing to do is go back out after the gold."

McKindrick was astonished. "You can't be serious. How can you prospect in your condition?"

"I don't need to prospect anymore."

"But you just said—"

"Let me finish." The prospector cut the trader off. "I didn't say go *find* gold. I'm goin' to go after the gold I already found."

"What?" McKindrick said.

This was news to Fargo, too. "You never mentioned finding any to me."

Pederson smiled. "I didn't know as I could trust you. And me blind and at your mercy." He shook his head. "No. It wouldn't have been smart."

McKindrick asked excitedly, "Are you saying you made a strike, Abner?"

"I'm sayin' I found what might be the richest damn vein in the whole damn territory," Pederson boasted. "But before I could do more than pinch myself and be sure I wasn't dreamin', I caught sight of Red Dog and his bucks. I got out of there, but with Mabel I couldn't go fast enough and they caught me. The rest you know."

"Excuse me for saying, but how in the world could you find it again? Blind as you are?"

"Why do you keep bringin' that up?"

"Sorry," McKindrick said. But he didn't sound sorry at all.

"Anyway," Pederson gruffly continued, "I figure I can find it again with some help. I know right where it is. All I need are a couple of people I trust to be my eyes."

"That's why you're sending for your relatives?"

"That would be one of the reasons," Pederson said.

"Is it possible you'll succeed?" McKindrick said, more to himself than to any of them.

"Why not?" Pederson demanded. "I know that country like the back of my hand. Every landmark. Every trail. Every water hole and tank. I'll guide them to it as easy as anything."

"I suppose you could, at that," McKindrick said. "I wonder, though, if there is as much gold as you claim."

"Are you callin' me a liar? I saw it with my own eyes, Abe. It will take three horses to pack it all out."

"Why, that would be a fortune. You'd be richer than Midas."

Pederson nodded. "I'll live the rest of my days bein' waited on hand and foot."

McKindrick poked at his stew, his bald pate knitted. "You'll need supplies, won't you? Horses, extra pack animals and the like. Do you have the money to buy all of that?"

"Well, no, but—"

"I have a proposition for you, then," the trader declared.

"I'm listenin'."

"I'll stake you," McKindrick said. "I'll give you everything you need in return, say, for a third of the gold you dig out."

"A third?" Pederson said. "That's a mighty big share."

"Horses and pack animals and tools don't come cheap. And I might lose every cent if you don't make it back. I think a third interest is more than fair given the risk I'm taking."

"I'm the one goin' back out into Apache country. Not you."

"All I ask is that you think about it."

Mary reached over and placed her hand on Pederson's arm. "Didn't losing your eyes teach you anything? I can't believe you're willing to put your life in peril again. To say nothing of the lives of your relatives."

"That's sweet of you, gal," Pederson said, "but you don't have to worry about how you're goin to make ends meet."

Mary glanced down the table and her jaw twitched. Coughing, she said, "How about you, Mr. Fargo? What's your opinion?"

"It's his hide," Fargo said. He smiled and winked. "All I care about is having fun."

7

Everyone was in bed, or supposed to be.

Fargo rose out of his and went to the door. He'd left it open a crack and now he opened it wider. The hall was empty. Slipping out, he went to the back door. The bolt didn't rasp. He stepped out and left the back door ajar.

Stars spanned the firmament and a sliver of moon added its feeble light. A mild breeze out of the north was welcome after the heat of the day.

Cemetery was dark. The trading post and saloon were black shapes against the night.

A coyote yipped, a signal for others to do the same, and soon the night pealed to the usual chorus.

Fargo went to the Ovaro and rubbed the stallion's neck. He stood leaning against a post and admiring the night for a good long while, and just when he figured he was wrong and she wouldn't show, the back door opened and out she came.

Mary McKindrick wore a robe tied at the throat. It accented the sweep of her breasts. She'd brushed her hair, and had pink slippers on her feet. She came over and stared at him. "Part of me wants to take an ax to you."

"Don't blame me," Fargo said. "No one is twisting your arm."

"I'm twisting my own." Mary sighed and gazed at the stars. Her eyes were shiny pools. "Life is never easy, is it?"

"You made your choice," Fargo said.

Mary's head snapped down. "That was cruel. Sometimes circumstances make us do things we might not do otherwise."

"No argument there," Fargo said to soothe her, and chuckled. "Is that what I am? A circumstance?"

"No. You've been a gentleman about it. A tease, but a gentleman." Mary sighed. "God, it feels wonderful to have a real man interested. I can't tell you."

"You're sure he'll stay asleep?"

"Are you kidding? Once Abe goes out, he stays out. The house could fall down around him and he wouldn't wake up. The drummer is a light sleeper, but even if he woke I doubt he'd say anything. He's afraid of you."

"Me?" Fargo said. "I've been as nice to him as I'd be to any chipmunk."

Mary smiled. "You have a way about you. An air, if you will."

"I wash more often than most men," Fargo said.

Mary laughed. "Yes, thank God. I've noticed that you don't stink. But the air you have is the same air a wolf has."

"Oh?"

"Anyone only has to take one look at you to know that if they give you trouble, they're in for it."

"Me?" Fargo said again. "I'm a daisy."

Mary continued to smile. "You are many things, I suspect, but a daisy isn't one of them." She folded her arms and stared at the house and then off across the wilds. "I've been thinking about where."

"We could dig a hole."

She laughed louder and caught herself. "Do you ever stop?"

"After a second or third helping," Fargo said.

"God, you excite me. You're not boring like someone I could name."

Before Fargo could stop himself he said, "You don't have to stay with him, you know."

"True," Mary said. "In time I'll have had enough, I suspect. Until then I live a life of quiet desperation, I guess you would call it."

"Life was meant for living."

"Are you sure you're a scout? You sound like my conscience in the lonely hours of the night."

"You're not alone now." Fargo stepped up to her. He didn't kiss her or touch her. He simply stood there, waiting.

Mary's throat bobbed. "Damn you."

"I'll take that as a compliment."

"What is it about you? Why are you so different from other men?"

"I put my pants on one leg at a time like they do."

"No," Mary said. "There's something I can't quite explain." She reached out almost shyly and traced his jaw with a fingertip. "I've had such wicked daydreams."

"I've had them, too, but I don't call them wicked."

"What are they, then?"

"Natural."

"You're good at this," Mary said. "You should give lessons."

"Good at what."

"Seduction."

"We still need the where," Fargo said.

"The last stall is empty."

Fargo took her hand and they walked along the long shed to the end farthest from the house. Even in the dark he could tell that fresh straw had been spread on the ground. ""Did you go to all this trouble just for me?"

"Don't flatter yourself," Mary said, and playfully smacked him on the shoulder.

Fargo cupped her bottom. "Whenever you're ready."

Suddenly Mary pressed against him, her mouth hungrily locked to his. She kissed him as if she were trying to suck him into her mouth. Her nails dug into his shoulders and her hips ground in slow circles. When she broke the kiss, she was panting.

"Nice," Fargo said.

"I had to get that out of my system," Mary said breathlessly.

"I hope there's more where that came from."

"A torrent."

Fargo pulled her into the stall and looped an arm around her waist. She smelled of lavender. He ran his hand through her hair and she gave a little shudder.

"Afraid?"

"No. I want it so much. So very, very much." She cupped his chin. "I want it to last."

"Until dawn is fine by me."

"I meant the memory to last," Mary said. "Besides, you said you're leaving at first light. How can you stay up all night and all day?"

"It depends on what keeps me up all night," Fargo said. He slowly pressed his mouth to hers and rimmed her lips with the tip of his tongue. Her mouth parted and their tongues danced. He cupped a breast and she melted into him, all resistance was gone. She unleashed the carnal tiger of her desires, and her hands were suddenly everywhere, exploring, caressing, groping.

Fargo moved onto the bed of straw. She willingly came with him, never breaking the kiss. Her robe was soft to the touch but couldn't compare to the softness of her skin.

He delved up and under and at the contact of his hand on her leg, she gasped. He ran his fingers up her inner thigh, almost to the junction, and she bit his lip and moaned and put her lips to his ear.

"I want you so much."

"I noticed."

"If you're not careful I'll eat you alive."

"I know where you can start," Fargo said, and placed her hand on his bulging manhood.

Mary sucked in her breath. "My God." She moved her hand up and down.

"It's been called other things," Fargo said.

She gripped his chin almost fiercely and looked him in the eye. "What *are* you?"

"Horny," Fargo said.

After that there was no more talk. They kissed and caressed and rubbed and stroked, and when her breaths were infernos and her thighs were molten to the touch, he undid the bow at the top of her robe and it parted and fell away to reveal that underneath she was naked. She was glorious: full, firm breasts, her nipples like tacks, sensitive to his mouth and his fingers. She arched her back and cooed and her legs opened and closed on his hand.

Mary pried at his buckle and got his gun belt off and set it aside. She plucked at his shirt and when it was loose, she slid her hand up and in and down.

Fargo's throat constricted when her questing fingers found

40

him. She stroked a few times and cupped him lower down, putting his will to the test.

Then they were both naked. Skin to skin, mouth to mouth. Fargo went near her mount of Venus but didn't touch it. Not yet. Not until her body hummed with need. Not until she was so ripe that when he brushed ever so lightly against her tiny knob, she about came up off the straw fit to explode.

"More," Mary begged. "Give me more."

She wasn't just wet for him. She was drenched. He inserted a finger and she lay still, breathless with her yearning. He pumped, and she clasped him and urged him to go harder and faster.

Few women had ever wanted him so much. She was true to her word; she sought to devour him. When she slid down his body, it was his turn to gasp.

Much later she was on her back and he was on his knees between her legs. He ran his tip along her slit, and her eyelids fluttered. He started to feed himself in and she choked off a cry. When he was sheathed to the hilt, her eyes widened.

"I never," she husked.

"You will," he said.

Their bodies blended into motion. He gripped her hips and rammed and rammed and she cooed in his ear, "Yes! Yes! Yes!"

Mary crested first. Her explosion seemed to shake the straw. She came and came, an orgasm so intense, it was a wonder she didn't break apart.

Fargo wasn't done. He let her lie quietly for a while and then he started anew. Her face reflected wonder.

"What are you?" she asked again.

"Almost there," Fargo said.

It wasn't long. She spurted a second time and this triggered his own release. It was as powerful as it always was, a potent drug he could never get enough of, more pleasurable than whiskey, than cards, than food, than anything short of breathing.

Fargo had never understood men who didn't like it, or were content with once a month. Why only have a sip when you could have the whole bottle?

Slick with sweat and nearly exhausted, they slowed and stopped and lay side by side, the breeze cool on their bodies.

"Magnificent," Mary breathed.

"I could say the same about you," Fargo said.

Mary languidly rolled against him and put her hand on his chest. "You know," she said, "if you should make it back this way after you're done with your business with the army, I'd gladly put you up for the night. I'd even pay for your room."

"Wench," Fargo said.

Mary laughed. "What can I say? You bring out the hussy in me." She sobered and caressed his neck. "Be careful out there. I don't want you to end up like poor Abner Pederson."

"Makes two of us," Fargo said.

8

It took nearly three weeks to find a site the major liked.

Fargo reached Apache Pass without incident. He camped two nights and on the third morning his patience was rewarded with the drum of hooves and the clatter of accoutrements.

Major Theodore Coult was an experienced officer. He had forty soldiers under him. After a base camp was set up, they roved the area seeking a suitable spot for the new fort. There had to be water. There had to be timber. It had to be somewhere the Apaches couldn't easily attack.

They finally settled on a site near a spring. There were woods. And from a nearby hill a lookout would be able to see for miles around and sound the alarm if Apaches appeared.

On the night before they were to part company, Fargo and the major and a sergeant sat around a crackling fire, drinking coffee.

"I can't thank you enough for your assistance," Major Coult remarked at one point.

"I didn't do much," Fargo said.

"On the contrary. You know this country better than just about anyone. Without you, it would have taken me months to find a site."

"How long before the fort is built?" Fargo idly asked.

"About a year, I should think. My report has to go through channels, and you know how slow that can go. They'll send a detachment to do the building. And afterward, the Tucson-Mesilla road will be a little bit safer."

"A little bit," Fargo said.

Major Coult frowned. "That's the best we can do where

Apaches are involved. I've fought the Blackfeet. I've fought the Sioux, or the Lakotas as some call them. I've fought Comanches in Texas. None of them put the fear of God in me like these damnable Apaches."

"They can do that."

"They're not like any Indians anywhere," Coult went on. "They're killers, through and through."

Fargo sipped and said, "They made this land theirs and now it's part of them. They resent whites trying to take it away."

"Hell, they resent everybody," Coult said. "Before they fought us they fought the Mexicans and before the Mexicans it was the Spanish and before that every other tribe they encountered. To them, killing is as natural as breathing."

"They're warriors," Fargo said.

"You almost sound as if you admire them."

Fargo leaned back on his saddle. "I admire anyone who does something well and they do what they do better than most."

The sergeant spoke up with "I don't see how you can admire a bunch of red savages. Didn't you hear what they did to those Mex freighters? Tied them to wagon wheels and set them on fire."

"Can you think of a better way to stop other freighters from coming through their land?"

"Now, hold on, Skye," Major Coult said. "We're talking atrocities. The Apaches don't just fight. They wage a war of extermination."

"No mercy," Fargo said, "ever."

"Yes," Major Coult said, "that pretty much sums it up. And it's hardly admirable."

"They'll get theirs," the sergeant declared. "It might take us years yet, but we'll whip them like we've whipped everybody else."

"You're a good soldier, Sergeant," Major Coult said.

Fargo gazed out over the benighted mountains. Yes, he supposed the army would eventually prevail. And yes, it was a good thing to stop the Apaches from slaughtering and stealing. But a part of him would be sad to see them tamed and forced onto reservations and made the same as every other tribe.

For that matter, Fargo hated to see the West itself tamed. It was happening slowly but it was happening. Farms and settlements were spreading westward from the Mississippi River. Towns and even cities were springing up where before there had been wilderness. Eventually, the West would become like the East, and he hoped to God he wasn't alive to see it happen.

"Your sentiments about the Apaches notwithstanding," Major Coult said, "I want to thank you again for your help. Where will you go from here?"

Fargo hadn't given it much thought, but now that he did, he said, "Cemetery, I reckon."

"That pile of dust?" the sergeant said. "What's that trader's name? The stupid bastard who built the place?"

"McKindrick."

Major Coult frowned. "I've met the man and can't say I was impressed. Although he did offer to keep an eye out for the rifles."

"Rifles?" Fargo said.

"We've gotten wind of a shipment of new rifles bound for Apache hands. So long as they could only get single-shot Sharps, it wasn't so bad. But if they get hold of a lot of repeaters, they'll be twice the problem they are now."

"Apaches take weapons from people they kill all the time."

"I know," Coult said. "But we think someone is out to sell them new Henrys. If so, the rifles could only come straight from the factory."

"McKindrick?"

"We thought of that," Coult said. "The army had his books examined. And no, he buys older rifles secondhand so he can resell them for a higher profit."

"That sounds like something he would do."

"We checked with the factories, too," Coult revealed. "They have no record of McKindrick ever buying a new rifle from them."

"So it's someone else," the sergeant said. "I'd like to find out who and wring their red-loving neck."

"If you hear anything," Major Coult said to Fargo, "let me know."

"I will," Fargo promised.

As was his habit, he was up at the crack of day. He bade the major good-bye and headed west, up over Apache Pass. He didn't stay on the road but cut cross-country toward Cemetery. He had a hankering to see a certain lady again.

The second evening, he came to a spring he knew of. He watered the Ovaro and led the stallion a good hundred yards off into a cluster of boulders. His precaution paid off. Along about midnight he smelled smoke. He stayed awake all night.

The morning light revealed ten Apaches camped at the spring. They were on foot. They moved on about half an hour after sunrise, loping to the northeast like two-legged wolves.

Fargo didn't budge until they were out of sight. He rode with extra care all day and all night and on into the next evening when the lights of Cemetery twinkled in the distance.

He arrived bone-weary and covered with dust. The saloon tempted him, but he rode on past to the boardinghouse. He went up to the door and took off his hat and knocked.

The smile that spread across Mary's face was as warm as the impulsive hug she gave him. Quickly stepping back, she glanced at the trading post and composed herself. "How nice to see you again, Mr. Fargo," she said formally.

"I was in the neighborhood," Fargo said. "Reckoned I might take a room for the night."

Mary looked as if she wanted to cry. "Would that I could," she said. "They're all taken. Abner Pederson's relatives showed up."

"How about if I camp in your backyard?" Fargo proposed. "I'll pay for a stall and oats for my horse."

"I'll ask Abe," Mary said. "It's his decision, not mine."

"It doesn't become you," Fargo said.

"What doesn't?"

"Licking his boots."

Mary's cheeks grew scarlet. "Very well," she said. "I'll make the decision myself. Yes, you may stay. Take your animal around back. And you can join us for supper, too. We eat in twenty minutes or so."

"I'm obliged, ma'am," Fargo said with a smile.

Mary bent toward him and whispered, "Are you as randy as the last time?"

"More," Fargo said.

"Good." Mary grinned. "Then I'll let you have the stall for half price. Abe be damned."

Fargo went through the routine of stripping his saddle and saddle blanket and watering and feeding the Ovaro. He was about done when Mary came out of the house carrying a washbasin filled with clean water, and a towel.

"Five minutes," she announced. "And you're in for a surprise."

"I am?" Fargo said, ogling her.

"Not me," Mary said, laughing. "Something else. Something you won't hardly believe." She playfully plucked at his shirt. "Just remember. You're here on my account."

Wondering what she meant, Fargo slapped the dust from his buckskins and washed up and combed his hair. He entered the house and heard voices.

They were all at the table.

Abe McKindrick rose and shook his hand. "I didn't expect to see you again so soon." He didn't sound particularly pleased.

"I was passing through," Fargo lied. He hardly noticed the trader. It was the others who interested him.

First there was Abner Pederson. The old prospector wore brown leather eye patches over both eyes, and had on new store-bought clothes. He'd shaved off his stubble and appeared to have gained a few pounds. "It's good to see you again," he said, and gave a snort. "Listen to me. Old habits are hard to break. I should say it's good to *hear* you again."

"You're looking well," Fargo said.

"I have cause to," Pederson said. "My kin have come to help me."

"So I see," Fargo marveled.

On either side of the old ore hound sat two young women. They were alike enough to be sisters. Both had corn silk hair and eyes as green as mountain pines. Their faces were the sun-browned complexions of country girls.

Their clothes were plain: shirts and pants, not dresses.

Their bodies, even though they were seated, suggested a supple vigor. In short, they were candy for the eyes, women most men would look at twice.

"I'd like you to meet my nieces," Pederson was proudly saying. "They're from Missouri, but wait until you hear their names." He indicated the one on his right. "This pretty gal is Virginia." He motioned at the other. "And this pretty gal is Carolina." He chuckled. "Their ma named them after states she'd been to."

"They came all this way to help you mend?" Fargo said with friendly smiles for both.

"Oh, we're goin' to do more than that, mister," Virginia said with a distinct twang.

Carolina nodded. "We're goin' to get rich and kill us some Apaches."

9

Fargo waited until after he'd sat and the food was passed around and everyone was eating to clear his throat and ask, "What was that about killing Apaches?"

Both sisters had been eyeing him, discreetly in Virginia's case, more openly in Carolina's.

It was Virginia who put down her fork and said, "I should think you'd be more interested in the rich part. Mr. McKindrick sure is."

"Now, now, Ginny," the trader said. "It's a return on my investment for outfitting you. Nothing more."

"Ginny is how I like to be called," Virginia informed Fargo. "My sister here likes to be called Carol."

"Both of us hate that we're called states," Carol chimed in. "Our ma shouldn't ought to have named us like she did."

"The killing Apaches?" Fargo prompted.

"Goodness, you gnaw on a bone," Ginny said.

Carol forked a string bean into her mouth and beamed. "Any Apaches that try to stop us are as good as dead."

Ginny nodded. "We're farm girls, mister. We spent a lot of our time in the woods growin' up. We can ride and we can shoot and we ain't afeared of nothin'."

"Nothin'," Carol confirmed.

Fargo said, "What are the Apaches going to try and stop you from doing?"

"Oh. That's right. We ain't told you that part." Carol chuckled. "Our uncle says they'll likely try and stop us from gettin' his gold."

"We can't have that," Ginny said.

Fargo looked at Abner, who went on eating serenely. "Pederson," he said. "Tell me you're not."

49

"I am," the prospector said.

"Did you lose your mind when you lost your eyes?"

"Here, now," Ginny said. "We won't have you take that tone with him."

"He's our favorite uncle," Carol said, "and he's offered to make us rich."

"His offer will make you dead," Fargo said. "You're from Missouri. What do you know about Apaches?"

"We're not dumb," Ginny said indignantly. "They're red-skins, like the Chocktaws and the Creeks and the Pawnees and such."

"Apaches aren't like any Indians you've ever come across."

"Oh, there you go. More of that spook talk," Carol said. "We heard it from that gent over to the saloon, too. And Miss Mary here. How these Apaches are supposed to be red terrors." She stabbed a finger at Fargo. "Well, let me tell you, mister. They're men, just like you and our uncle. They're men and they bleed and we'll make them bleed bad if they give us trouble."

"Hell," Fargo said.

"You don't want us to do it because we're females," Ginny said.

"We can hold our own with any man, by God," Carol huffed.

Pederson raised his glass of water and swallowed. "Ahhh." He set the glass down. "Aren't my nieces somethin'?"

"You can't do this to them," Fargo said.

"It's not as if there's a law against it."

"You know what I mean."

"You're forgettin' somethin', Fargo," Pederson said. "You're forgettin' all the times I've made it out there and back and nothin' ever happened to me."

"All it takes is once," Fargo said while staring at the eye patches.

"And all I need is one more," Pederson said. "I know the landmarks. I can guide them. We'll slip in and load up our pack animals with the gold and slip out again. I'll split it with my nieces and they'll take me to Missouri and help me buy a place where I can sit on a rockin' chair the rest of my days and be waited on hand and foot."

Carol folded her hands under her chin and regarded Fargo with amusement. "We hear tell you're partial to a Henry."

"What does that have to do with anything?"

"We have Henrys, too," Ginny said.

"And we can shoot flies off a fence at twenty paces," Carol declared.

"Any Apaches come near us, we'll put out their eyes like they did our uncle's," Ginny vowed.

Fargo saw that trying to talk them out of it was a waste of breath. And Abner certainly wouldn't listen to reason. That left the trader. "You're willing to outfit them knowing they might not make it back?"

McKindrick sniffed. "They happen to be adults and can do as they please. And Mr. Pederson has offered to pay me twice what it will cost me for supplies and the horses they need. Plus I get a third interest in any gold they bring back. I'd be a fool to decline."

Mary hadn't said anything in a while, but now she did. "All you care about is the money."

McKindrick's head snapped up and his beady eyes glittered. "Have a care, my dear. I won't be talked down to, especially at my own table."

"I'm sorry, Abner," Mary said, "but it's wrong."

"You have no business sense, my dear," McKindrick said. "But then, you're a woman, after all."

Fargo sensed that Mary controlled herself with an effort. To distract McKindrick he said, "Here's an idea. Why not ask the army for an escort, Abner?"

Pederson laughed coldly. "Oh, sure. Take soldiers to my gold. What's to stop them from killin' me and the girls and keepin' it for themselves?"

"Not everyone is as greedy as you."

"Greed, hell," Pederson said. "A man has to live, doesn't he? Now that I've lost my sight, I need money more than ever."

"Quit pickin' on our uncle," Carol said.

"He's done us a favor askin' for our help," Ginny said.

Carol nodded. "He knows how much we'd like to leave the farm and go off and live in the big city."

"Any big city," Ginny confirmed.

"With the gold we can," Carol said. "We'll have pretty dresses and be proper ladies and all."

"We're all set to head out," Ginny said.

Carol nodded. "Tomorrow at noon."

Long ago Fargo had learned that there was no talking sense to idiots. He finished his meal and excused himself and went out back. The stars were sparkling and the night wind was cool. He spread out his blankets in the empty stall at the far end and debated what to do.

Over an hour went by and he drifted off. A soft sound woke him. He opened his eyes and smelled perfume and smiled. "How do you do, ma'am?"

Mary was in her robe with the tie at the throat. She sank to her knees, put her hands on his chest, and hungrily kissed him. "Everyone is asleep."

"Good." Fargo pulled her to him.

When they broke for breath Mary whispered, "Thank you for coming back."

"I wanted a second helping."

"Of my food or me?"

"Both."

This time Fargo took his time. She was soft and yielding and eager to gush and did so twice before he eventually went over the brink. They drifted to a tired stop with her head on his chest and his hand in the small of her back.

"That was nice."

"You're wasting yourself on a man like him," Fargo stated bluntly.

"I know. But without Abe I'd be struggling to make ends meet. I guess you could say I've traded my heart for peace of mind."

Fargo didn't say any more. It was her life.

"How about your own heart?"

"I don't think about it much."

"You've mentioned how much you love scouting and exploring and the like. You won't let anything or anyone tie you down. You've traded a hearth and a home for your wanderlust."

"I suppose I have," Fargo admitted.

"I envy you," Mary said softly.

Fargo changed the subject. "What do you make of this Pederson business?"

"Him going after the gold with his nieces?" Mary rested her chin on her hands and gazed admiringly into his eyes. "I think he's asking for an early grave and he'll take them with him."

"I think the same."

"But what can anyone do? He has his mind made up and those two think they can lick any Apaches they come across. The poor deluded dears. I would never take Apaches for granted."

"There's never a shortage of stupid," Fargo said.

Mary laughed. "I don't know if Ginny and Carol are stupid so much as overconfident. They can ride like anything. And they're marvelous shots. I watched them practice. They can hit bottles at a hundred yards ten times out of ten."

"Apaches aren't bottles."

"I guess they'll have to learn that the hard way."

Fargo sighed.

"You're thinking of helping them, aren't you?"

"Pederson might not want my help."

"But you're thinking of helping them anyway. I know you well enough by now."

"Oh?" Fargo said, and touched her chin. "After you've had your way with me two times?"

Mary grinned and pecked him. "I'd have my way with you a thousand times if you let me. But yes. I saw you at the table. You would save them from getting themselves killed if you could."

Fargo grunted.

"What I don't get is why," Mary said. "What are they to you?"

"Nothing."

"Yet you'd risk your life for theirs? There has to be a reason."

"It beats being bored."

"Oh, Skye," Mary said. "It's the women, isn't it? You're thinking of all the horrible things the Apaches might do to them."

"You talk too much," Fargo said.

"A female failing, they say," Mary teased. She sat up. "I suppose I'd better get back to bed. I just wish I had you to cuddle with." She tied her robe and bent and kissed him passionately.

"What was that for?"

"To remember me by. And to invite you back anytime you want. Anytime at all." Mary stepped to the open end of the stall and looked back, her figure a dark silhouette.

"Do me a favor, handsome. Don't get yourself killed on their account."

"I'll try not to," Fargo said.

10

Fargo couldn't say what woke him. It was the middle of the night, about three judging by the positions of the stars. He lay there and listened and didn't hear anything. He was on the verge of falling back to sleep when the Ovaro nickered.

Fargo slid out from under his blankets with his Colt in his hand. He crept to the end of the stall.

The yard was empty, the house was still.

He moved along the horse shed to the Ovaro. The stallion had its ears pricked and was sniffing. Its head was toward the trading post.

Crossing to a corner of the house, Fargo peered around. The trading post, too, was quiet and dark. But the stallion was seldom wrong. He waited, and before long figures appeared: riders, slowly approaching the building from the side.

It was a good fifty yards from the house to the post. He couldn't possibly cross that much open space without being spotted. He had to content himself with watching as the riders came up to the side door. One dismounted and seemed to be trying to force it open.

Another of the riders came toward the front of the post and out from the shadows into the starlight. He stared at the saloon and then at the house, apparently to satisfy himself that no one was up and about.

It was an Apache.

Fargo raised his Colt. They were trying to break in, he reckoned. Probably after guns. He took aim at the warrior who had ridden into the open, but the man reined around and rejoined his companions.

Fargo took a gamble. Hunching low to the ground, he

sprinted toward the post. All it would take was for one of them to glance in his direction. Miraculously, he made it.

He put his back to the wall and sidled to the corner and poked his head out.

The side door was open. Several Apaches were filing inside.

He had to stop them. The more guns they got their hands on, the more whites they'd kill. He centered the Colt on a squat form on a pinto, thumbed back the hammer, and fired.

The warrior tumbled over the back of the pinto as if kicked by a mule.

Fargo thumbed back the hammer, fired again. An arrow thudded into the wall inches from his face. A rifle boomed and a slug whizzed past his hat. He fired a third time and another warrior clutched himself and threw an arm over his mount's neck to keep from falling off.

The warriors who had gone in came running out. More rifles banged. Repeaters sprayed lead.

Fargo was forced to duck back. He only had two pills left in the wheel. If they rushed him, he was a goner. Fingers flying, he replaced the spent cartridges. Hooves drummed, and he looked out.

They were racing away.

He raised the Colt, but another rifle cracked and splinters stung his cheek. He jerked back, then sent two shots after them.

Shouts came from the house. Lights were coming on there and at the saloon.

The Apaches melted into the night.

Fargo warily approached the one he had shot. To his surprise, the warrior was still alive. He was breathing in ragged gasps and dark drops flecked his mouth and chin. He wasn't long for this world. "*Shis-Inday,*" Fargo said. It was the Apache name for themselves. It meant, "men of the woods."

The warrior's eyes fixed on him. "*Pindah lickoyee, tu no vale nada.*" Which was a mix of Chiricahua and Spanish for "White-eyed man, you are good for nothing."

Fargo had to respect a man who could spit out an insult at death's door. "You are the one who is dying," he said.

The warrior grunted.

"It is not like the Apache to be so careless," Fargo said.

"I follow Red Dog," the warrior said, as if that explained everything.

"And Red Dog was after guns," Fargo said.

The warrior said a strange thing. "He trusts your kind. I do not. All white-eyes have two tongues." He coughed and more blood dribbled from his mouth.

"Red Dog would never trust a white."

The warrior said another strange thing. "He knows you have bad hearts. He trusts that."

Fargo sank to a knee. He kept his Colt trained on the warrior. Even weak and almost dead, Apaches were deadly dangerous. "Would you like me to take your body and bury it after you are *tats-an*?"

"You would do that for me?"

"I have no hate for the Apache."

"I have hate for your kind. You try to take our land. You want it for your own."

Fargo didn't say anything.

"You would really bury me?"

"*Shee-dah*," Fargo said.

"Then maybe you are not as much my enemy as other white-eyes."

"How are you known?" Fargo asked.

"*Too-ah-yay-say*."

"Strong Swimmer."

"You know our tongue?"

"I know some," Fargo said. He had a smattering of a dozen tongues, and more than a smattering of others.

Strong Swimmer gazed at the sky. "I did not think to die this way. You took me by surprise."

"There were many of you and I was one."

Strong Swimmer grunted. "A warrior kills any way he can."

And with that, he died.

Fargo knelt there staring as hurried footsteps approached. When he looked up he was surrounded; Abe McKindrick was there, Mary in her robe, Ginny and Carol in shirts and britches hastily thrown on, each holding one of Abner Pederson's hands, and the man who ran the saloon and lived in a room at the back, holding a shotgun.

"An Apache!" the latter exclaimed. "Right smack in the middle of town."

Fargo gazed at the pitifully few buildings and refrained from laughing.

"You killed him," McKindrick said. He sounded horrified.

"They broke into your trading post," Fargo said, and nodded at the open side door.

"Oh God," McKindrick said.

"How many were there?" Mary asked.

"Seven or eight," Fargo said. "Their leader was Red Dog."

"Oh God," McKindrick said again.

Ginny let go of Abner and nudged the body with a toe. "You did right good, mister. They say the only good redskin is a dead redskin."

"Ain't that the truth?" Carol echoed.

McKindrick put his hand to his forehead. "This is awful. Just awful."

"They were only inside a couple of minutes. I doubt they stole much," Fargo lied. He was sure that when they came out, they had repeaters. Yet when he was in the post last, he hadn't seen any on display.

"No, that's not—" McKindrick stopped and shook himself. "I guess I better go see." He bustled inside, muttering.

"What's the matter with him?" the saloon owner asked.

Abner chortled. "He's probably worried they found his strongbox."

Fargo didn't think that was it.

Ginny reached behind her and produced a knife. "Move aside, mister. I'd like one of those ears as a keepsake."

"What?" Mary said.

"You heard me," Ginny replied. "I'll salt it and stick it on a thong and wear it around my neck."

"That's"—Mary couldn't seem to think of a suitable word—"barbaric."

"It's nothin' compared to what redskins do to white folks," Carol said.

Ginny motioned at Fargo. "Move aside, I said. I have cuttin' to do."

"No."

In the act of bending, Ginny stopped. "What did you say?"

"He stays in one piece."

Ginny straightened. "The hell you say. Why do you care if I take an ear?"

"I gave him my word I'd see to his body."

Carol said, "You did what?"

"You heard me." Fargo stood. "His name was Strong Swimmer. In the morning I'm taking him off into the hills and burying him."

"You know his name?" Carol said.

Fargo holstered his Colt.

"Buryin' an Apache," Ginny said. "That's about the stupidest notion I ever heard. But I'm still takin' an ear."

"No," Fargo said, "you're not."

Ginny wagged the knife at him. "There's one thing you better learn, mister. When me and my sister want to do somethin', we do it. Now out of my way." She pushed him and started to reach down.

Fargo slugged her. He drove his fist into her gut, seized her wrist, and wrenched the knife from her grasp.

Doubled over, she staggered.

"Hey!" Carol cried, and produced a knife of her own. "You leave my sister be, you hear?"

"Stop this," Mary said. "Get a hold of yourself."

"Stay out of this," Carol said, and came at Fargo with her knife poised to thrust.

Fargo had had enough. He flashed the Colt out and cocked it before she could blink. At the *click* of the hammer, she stopped.

"You wouldn't," Carol said.

"Try me."

"Most men wouldn't shoot a female. It goes against their grain."

Fargo held the Colt rock steady.

"They put us on pedestals," Carol went on, "and think we're too special to hurt."

"I put women in beds and do what comes natural," Fargo said.

Despite herself, Carol grinned. "I don't quite know what to make of you."

"Put the knife away."

Carol obeyed.

Ginny had stopped sputtering and was glaring at him. "I won't forget this. I surely won't."

Fargo threw her knife at her feet. "Stick it in your sheath and get the hell out of here."

Scowling, Ginny, too, complied. She took Abner's hand and said, "Come on, Uncle. The air here has gotten rank."

Carol stared after them and said, "My sis ain't the forgivin' sort. You've made an enemy here tonight, mister."

"I'll try not to lose sleep over it," Fargo said.

11

But he did. The rest of the night, Fargo didn't sleep more than half an hour at a time. He tried, but he'd wake up troubled. He couldn't stop thinking about those repeaters. And about where the Apaches had gotten them.

Before daybreak he was up and saddled the Ovaro. He needed an extra horse to take the body and was going to wait for Mary to be up and about and ask her if he could use one of theirs. Then he noticed a light was on in the trading post, and a shadow moved across the window. He went over and around to the side door, and knocked. He happened to glance at the lock. It was in one piece and had no scratch marks.

Abe McKindrick's eyes were bloodshot and he was gnawing on his lip when he opened it. "You," he said with no enthusiasm.

"I'm off to bury the Apache," Fargo informed him. "I'd like to borrow a horse. I'll have it back by noon."

"Why not make it easy for yourself and bury him out back?"

"I gave him my word."

"What's a promise to a heathen?" McKindrick said.

"Don't you start," Fargo warned.

McKindrick did more gnawing. "Sure. Take the sorrel. Try not to let anything happen to him. This night has been enough of a disaster."

"What did they steal?"

"Eh?"

"They must have stolen something if it's a disaster." Fargo used his own word.

"Oh. No. You interrupted them before they could take more than"—the trader hestitated—"a few trinkets."

Fargo simmered. But he didn't let on. "There's no predicting Apaches."

"No," McKindrick said, and gazed worriedly into the distance. "There isn't. Well, I have work to do." He shut the door.

Fargo examined the jamb. The wood around the door was untouched. He nodded, and returned to the horse shed for the sorrel. He led it from the stall and was climbing on the Ovaro when the back door opened and out came Mary. She was dressed and looked as pretty as the dawn. "Morning, ma'am," he said with a grin. "The grump over at the trading post gave me permission to borrow your horse."

Mary didn't smile. She was wringing her hands. "I came out to warn you," she said quietly. "You should have heard them talking last night."

"Ginny and Carol," Fargo guessed.

"Ginny was as mad as a wet hornet," Mary said. "She truly means to do you harm."

"I was hoping she had more brains."

"How can you take it so calmly? I overheard them say that they've shot people before. Knifed a few, too."

"Tough ladies," Fargo said.

Mary frowned. "I wish you'd be more serious about this. She's liable to stick a blade in your back."

"If I turn my back to her, I deserve it."

"The other sister was trying to get her to forget about it. They still intend to leave today. Once they're gone, you'll be safe."

"Those girls are from Missouri."

"What difference does that make?"

"Missourians are good haters and believe in the feud."

"You almost sound as if that's a good thing," Mary said.

"I believe in an eye for an eye myself. And I'm not fond of two-legged sheep."

"I'm not sure I follow. I was raised to turn the other cheek. To accept what life throws our way without complaint."

"And now you're living with a man you don't love in the middle of nowhere with nothing to do all day but rock in a chair and knit."

Mary flinched. "There you go, being cruel again," she said, her voice breaking.

"Sometimes the truth hurts."

"You're not in my shoes," Mary said. "You don't understand."

"I'd never let myself be in your shoes. Neither would those girls from Missouri."

"How can you talk to me like this? After all we've shared? And for your information, I have been taking steps to strike off on my own." Abruptly wheeling, Mary went back in, her back as stiff as an ironing board.

"I handled that well," Fargo said to the Ovaro, and tugged on the lead rope. As he was passing the front of the house, he spotted a face glaring at him from an upstairs window. It was Ginny. He smiled and gave a cheery little wave. She raised a hand to her throat and ran a finger along it as if slitting it with a knife. He mimed drawing his Colt and pointing it at her and shooting. Her lips curled down and she snapped the curtains closed. He chuckled and rode over to the trading post.

Strong Swimmer was heavy. It took some doing because the sorrel didn't like the smell of blood, but Fargo got him up and over, belly down. As he was climbing back on the Ovaro, the trading post door opened.

McKindrick stared glumly at the body. "I wish you hadn't killed him."

"I was trying to stop them from stealing your guns."

"Red Dog might blame me," McKindrick said anxiously. "He has a temper, that one. And he hates whites more than he hates anything."

"I've made the man's acquaintance," Fargo reminded him.

"Well, if you should run into him, be sure and tell him this was your doing."

"I doubt he'll want to pass the time of day." Fargo got out of there before he said something he shouldn't. Not yet, anyway.

For an hour or so the air was cool and the ride was pleasant. Then the temperature climbed and it was like riding in an oven.

Fargo was making for a spur that cut half a mile into the plain. A gradual climb brought him to a rocky ridge.

He searched and found a spot amid high boulders. He'd brought a shovel that had been leaning against the shed and it wasn't long before he had a grave dug. He slid the body off the sorrel and placed it in the hole and folded the warrior's arms across his chest. To fill it in only took a minute. He piled rocks as a precaution against scavengers and was about to climb back on the Ovaro when he heard the clatter of hooves from below.

Thinking it might be Apaches, he shucked the Henry from his saddle scabbard and cat-footed to a flat rock that overlooked his back trail.

Ginny and Carol were climbing the ridge. Both had Henrys of their own.

Fargo let them come. They were intent on his tracks and now and then scanned the crest but didn't spot him. When they were within earshot, he wedged his rifle to his shoulder and slid farther out and called down, "That's far enough, ladies."

They drew rein and glanced up. Ginny started to jerk her Henry but thought better of it. Carol merely grinned.

Fargo didn't see anything funny about being stalked.

"I should shoot you both."

"But you won't," Ginny said confidently.

"How's your belly?" Fargo asked.

"Hittin' a woman is one thing. Shootin' a woman is another."

"I don't put females on pedestals, remember?"

"Even so." Ginny leaned on her saddle horn. "Prove me wrong. Gun me in cold blood."

Carol laughed.

"We can be patient," Ginny said. "You caught us this time. But what about the next? Or the time after that? Sooner or later I'll catch you unawares and that will be that."

"You come right out with it."

"Mister, no one treats me like you did and gets away with it."

"The smart thing is to let it drop."

"You're sayin' I'm dumb?" Ginny colored. "You just pile them on."

"Turn around and go back," Fargo said. "And tell your uncle for me that he's a fool."

"Mister, I wouldn't lift a finger for you. Tell my uncle your own self." Angrily wheeling her mount, Ginny headed down.

Carol was still grinning. "It's a cryin' shame," she said.

"What is?"

"A handsome fella like you. If'n Ginny hadn't taken it into her head to buck you out in gore, I might have let you have a poke."

"Talk sense to her," Fargo said.

Carol laughed. "Have you been payin' attention? My sis is as hardheaded as they come. Once she sets her mind to somethin', there ain't no changin' it." She sighed. "I reckon I'll never have that poke now." She raised her reins.

"Carol," Fargo said.

She looked up.

"You're in over your heads. I'm saying this for your own good, not as an insult. If the Apaches get their hands on you, they might stake you out and peel your skin."

"It won't work," Carol said, chuckling. "We don't scare easy."

"Damn it, woman," Fargo said. "Are you hankering to die?"

"Apaches are men. Nothin' more, nothin' less. They bleed. They die. We'll do to them as we'd do to any others."

"You're as hardheaded as your sister."

Carol regarded him thoughtfully. "Listen, mister. I don't have a grudge against you like my sis does. Fact is, I sort of like you. And I savvy you're sayin' all that to spare us from bein' hurt, or worse."

"But?" Fargo said.

"But we gave our word we'd help our uncle Abner, and once we give our word, we don't go back on it."

"Damn it."

"There's somethin' else," Carol said.

"The gold."

She nodded. "Ginny and me will have more money than we'll know what to do with. It'll be like a dream."

"Or a nightmare."

Carol acted as if she hadn't heard him. "All our lives we've been dirt poor. The clothes on our backs was all we had growin' up, and the clothes were hand-me-downs. This horse and this new rifle? Uncle Abner sent us the money for them so we could come help him."

"What you're telling me," Fargo said, "is that there's nothing I can say or do that will change your mind."

"My sis and me mean to see this through, come what may."

"Even if you lose your life?"

Carol laughed and reined around and said over her shoulder, "No one lives forever."

12

Their tracks were plain to follow during the day, and at night the glow of their fire told him where they were camped. It would tell the Apaches, too. Fargo thought Pederson had more sense. Maybe the old man didn't realize his nieces made their fire too big.

The third night out Fargo made camp in a dusty bowl that hid his own small fire from prying eyes. He put coffee on to perk and climbed to the top of the bowl to scour the countryside as he did every night.

The only glow was the Pederson fire. But then, Apaches wouldn't make the same mistake the nieces made. Apache fires, like his, would be well hidden.

The wail of a coyote commenced the usual refrain. He sat and listened to the ululating cries and sipped his coffee and wondered why in hell he was doing this. The sisters were nothing to him. He hardly knew them. But he knew what the Apaches might do to them if they were taken captive.

Then there was the other thing: Red Dog's visit to the trading post had kindled a suspicion.

Fargo grinned at the irony. Here he was, the last man in the world to want to see the West settled and more towns and cities spread everywhere. Yet he was out to stop the culprit who was supplying rifles to the Apaches, who would stop that spread.

Life was too damn silly for words.

That was when the Ovaro raised its head and pricked its ears.

Quietly setting the tin cup down, Fargo slicked his Colt and crept to the top of the bowl. Lower down, and to his left, pebbles clattered. Something—or someone—was down there. They weren't after him, though. The chink of a hoof on stone told him they were heading north—in the direction of the Pederson fire.

Fargo strained for a glimpse. He would bet his poke it was Apaches. Few other tribes dared venture into their territory.

He stayed up late listening for war whoops and gunfire, but the night proved uneventful.

At first light he was in the saddle and descended in search of sign. He found it, and a mystery.

Four riders had passed by in the dead of night, and all four rode shod horses.

Fargo sat his saddle and scratched his chin in puzzlement. Shod horses usually meant whites. And it was rare for whites to venture this far in. He decided to follow the sign awhile, and he soon discovered that the four riders were doing the same thing he was: they were shadowing the Pedersons.

It didn't bode well for the old prospector and the sisters.

Fargo stayed on their trail. They were hanging well back so they wouldn't be spotted, confirming his hunch that they were up to no good.

Toward sundown their tracks pointed toward a jumble of giant boulders and slabs.

Fargo drew rein in shadow. He dismounted and rested until the sun had set. Then he took his rifle and advanced on foot.

He placed each boot with care. The slightest sound would give him away.

Smoke tingled his nose. Sinking flat, he crawled until he saw a fire. There were three of them. The fourth horse must be a pack animal. They'd collected dry grass and droppings and were roasting a lizard. They were also passing a bottle back and forth.

Their clothes, the fact that each was an armory, pegged them as border ruffians. Predators who preyed on the weak and the unwary. As dangerous in their own right as the Apaches.

The biggest and the oldest, who had to be in his forties, was going on about something or other.

Fargo snaked nearer. He'd like to hear what they were saying.

". . . be like takin' oatmeal from an infant," the man was saying. He swigged from the bottle, and chuckled. "It fell in our lap, this one did."

"So you hope, Nash," said one of the younger ones. He favored black clothes and black boots and wore a pearl-handled Smith & Wesson, butt forward, on his hip.

"Here, now, boy," Nash said.

"Don't call me that."

"You're too prickly, Lucian," Nash said. "You have to learn to take life easy, like me."

The other young one wore a brown hat and vest. His six-shooter was a Starr. At the moment he was adding dry brush to the flames. "I still can't get over that old fool gabbin' like he did."

"Pederson didn't know we were there, Stokes," Nash said. "Or didn't you see those eye patches?"

"Blind or not, I wouldn't brag to a barkeep that I'd struck it rich and was headin' out after the gold," Stokes said.

Fargo mentally swore. So that was it. Pederson had gone to the saloon for a drink and told the bartender his plans. And these three had overheard him.

"Be grateful he was so stupid," Nash said, "or we wouldn't know about the gold ourselves."

"I can't wait to get my hands on it."

"But wait you will," Nash said. "We let them lead us to it. We let them dig it out. And when they're done, we take their packs and plant them and head for Mexico."

Lucian said, "I like all that except the Mexico part. You can live out the rest of your days with a bunch of burrito eaters but not me. I'm takin' my share and headin' for St. Louis or maybe New Orleans."

"What would you do in a city?" Nash said. "They have law, remember?"

"Tin stars don't scare me."

"That's the trouble," Nash said. "Nothin' scares you. Not even Apaches."

"And they should," Stokes said.

"I've yet to meet the hombre, white or red or any other color, who's faster than me," Lucian bragged.

"Apaches don't have to be fast with a six-shooter," Nash said. "They'll shoot you in the back. Or slit your throat while you're sleepin'."

"They'll try."

Nash got back to the original subject with "Stokes is right, though, about Pederson bein' a fool. To think. Bringin' two pretty fillies like those nieces of his into Apache country."

"It's a damn shame," Stokes said. "You know what the Apaches will do to them."

"I surely do," Nash said.

"He must not care for them much."

"Or he cares for the gold a whole hell of a lot more," Nash said.

"Or it could be his brain ain't all there," Lucian remarked.

The other two looked at him.

"He had his eyes dug out of their sockets," Lucian elaborated. "That would drive anyone loco."

"You think he brought them out here because he ain't thinkin' straight?" Nash said. "Could be, I reckon. But he never was all there to begin with. I've seen him around. You have to be half crazy to look for gold in these mountains."

"We're in these mountains," Stokes said.

"We have a reason to be," Nash said. "We're not wanderin' all over, pokin' at the ground, like he used to do."

Stokes glanced nervously into the dark. "I hope those red devils don't latch on to us."

Lucian patted his Starr revolver. "They do and they'll wish they hadn't."

"Listen to yourself," Nash said.

"What?"

"We keep tellin' you that fightin' Apaches ain't like fightin' anyone else. You'll have to find that out the hard way, I reckon."

"We have an edge," Lucian said. "It shouldn't ought to come to that."

"Thank God," Stokes said.

Nash raised his head. "Speakin' of which, where in hell did he get to?"

"He went off to answer nature, I reckon," Stokes responded.

"He should have been back by now."

Fargo tensed. So there *were* four of them. He started to twist his head to scour the vicinity when a hard object gouged the nape of his neck.

"You move," a hard, low voice said quietly, "you die."

Fargo froze.

"We do this slow," the voice said. "I tell you to do something, you do it. You don't, you die. Savvy?"

"Savvy," Fargo said.

"Good. Slide your rifle as far out from you as it will go."

Fargo did.

"Take your hand off the rifle."

Fargo did.

"Put both your hands in front of you and get to your knees. Any tricks, you die."

Fargo had seldom been so impressed by just a voice. He knew that if he so much as twitched wrong, the gun against his neck would go off. He did as he was told.

"You are my dog," the voice said, sounding amused. "Hold your arms out from your sides, dog."

Once more, Fargo did exactly as he was told. He felt movement at his holster and glanced down. He had been relieved of his Colt.

"I am called Scarface," the voice said. "Perhaps you have heard of me."

Fargo swore.

The man behind him laughed. "You have, then. Tell me. What have you heard?"

"That your mother was a Mescalero Apache," Fargo recollected. "That she was raped by drunken whites. That she gave birth and you were what came out, and her people wanted nothing to do with you. Neither did the whites."

"Breeds are hated by red and white," Scarface said. "But that is all right. I hate them as much as they hate me."

"It's said you've killed a lot of people."

"A lot. But the hate has nothing to do with it. I kill because I like to kill." Scarface gouged the muzzle deeper. "Now you will tell me who you are."

Fargo saw no reason not to give his real name.

There was silence, and then Scarface said, "You speak with a straight tongue?"

"Why would I lie?"

"Your name is known to me. They say you are one of the best white scouts. They say you have lived with the Sioux and other tribes. Even the Apaches hold you in high regard."

This was news to Fargo. "What now?"

"We go see my friends at the fire."

"How can whites be your friends?" Fargo stalled. He was trying to think of a way to turn the tables without being shot.

"I ride with them because it suits my purpose. Now do not talk again unless I say you can."

Fargo bit off a reply.

"Keep doing as you are told," Scarface said, "and you will live longer. But not too long, eh?"

13

Fargo was prodded into the firelight at gunpoint. His every instinct was to whirl and get out of there. He didn't. His instincts would get him dead.

Nash and Stokes leaped to their feet in surprise. Lucian stayed seated, grinning.

"Scarface!" Nash blurted. "What do we have here?"

"You have eyes."

The breed gave Fargo a push and Fargo stumbled and almost fell.

Stokes clawed at his six-shooter and leveled it. "I've got him covered, pard."

"A little late, you idiot," Scarface said. "And I'm not your goddamned pard."

"I didn't know he was out there," Stokes said.

"My point," Scarface said.

"What was he doin?" Nash asked.

"Spying on you three."

Fargo still hadn't seen his captor. He did now, as Scarface stepped around to the other side of the fire and squatted.

The notorious killer of over twenty men, women, and—some said—children was as thin as a rake handle. He wore buckskins that had seen a lot of use. He also wore Apache-style knee-high moccasins and the kind of headband that Apaches favored. His face, bronzed by long exposure to the sun, bore three scars: one across the forehead, another that split his left cheek, and a third that gave him a cleft jaw. Sword strokes, unless Fargo missed his guess, from a run-in with a cavalryman. His eyes were a startling green.

"Like what you see, Fargo?" Scarface said, and laughed.

"That's his name?" Nash asked. "What do we do with him?"

"You do nothing," Scarface said. "He's mine."

Lucian said, "You sure do put on airs."

Scarface fixed those penetrating green eyes on him. "A thing to remember," he said coldly, "is that no one has ever insulted me and lived."

"I'm only sayin'," Lucian said, not the least bit intimidated.

"You will say yourself to death one day."

"Maybe so." Lucian grinned. "But I'll go out in a way folks will remember."

Scarface looked at Fargo. "Do you see what I am stuck with?"

"Hey, now," Nash said.

"This captive of mine is famous," Scarface said. "You might have heard of him, but I doubt it since you are like most whites and dumb to the world around you."

"The way you talk," Stokes said.

"He has been following the old prospector," Scarface went on. "He saw the fire I told you to make where no one can see, and came to find out who you were."

"Damn," Fargo said. It was obvious the breed had been on to him for some time now.

Nash had the same thought. "How long have you known he's been following Pederson and those gals?"

"Since yesterday morning when I cut his trail while I was out looking for sign of Apaches."

"And you didn't think to tell us?"

"There is a lot I do not tell you," Scarface said.

"I thought we were friends."

Scarface grinned at Fargo. "There's that word again." To Nash he said, "You thought wrong. We ride together because you like to steal and I like to kill. So you rob people and I kill them to keep them from telling others you robbed them. It works out well, eh?"

"Full of yourself," Lucian said.

Fargo was being ignored. He was tempted to bolt, but he doubted he'd get three feet before Scarface put a slug into him.

"What are you fixin' to do with him?" Nash asked.

"I haven't decided yet," Scarface said. "I might cut on him awhile. They say he is tough and I would like to see how tough."

"He doesn't look so tough to me," Lucian said.

Scarface grinned at Fargo. "And they say breeds have no brains."

Fargo had to laugh.

"But I will not cut on him now," Scarface said to Nash. "Sounds carry at night. The prospector might hear. Or Apaches who might be near. So maybe I will kill him outright."

"Get to it, then," Nash said.

"When I'm ready."

"We can't just have him standin' there," Nash objected.

"True. Tie him."

"You caught him. You should tie him."

"Tie him anyway."

"Why should I?"

"Because I said so."

"Full of himself up to here," Lucian said, and put a hand to his chin.

Nash turned red. "Damn it, Scarface. We let you join us because folks say you're so good at killin'. Not so you can boss us around."

"You let me?" Scarface said, and snorted. "You begged me. I am of more use to you than either of these." He motioned at Lucian and Stokes. "As for my captive, tie him to show me you know how to do something right."

"You're goin' too far," Nash said.

"Am I? Who made the fire where it can be seen? Who was being spied on and had no idea? He could have shot you dead if not for me."

Nash scowled. "I do my best, but I'm not you." He turned to Stokes. "Tie him."

"Why me?"

"Because he wants it done and I told you to."

Lucian chortled. "They know better than to ask me to do it."

"I don't much like always bein' the lowest man on this

totem pole," Stokes complained. But he got a rope and cut off a suitable length and came around behind Fargo. "Put your hands behind you. No funny business, you hear?"

"That's the way," Scarface said. "Make him tremble in fear."

"Bein' afeared of Stokes," Lucian said, "is like bein' afeared of a pup or a kitten."

"Go to hell, both of you," Stokes said.

Nash was studying Fargo. "Why are you followin' that old goat? Are you after the gold, too?"

"Of course he is," Lucian said.

"Anyone with any brains would be," Stoke chipped in as he looped rope around Fargo's wrists.

"So few brains," Scarface said.

Stokes stopped tying and poked his head past Fargo. "How's that again?"

"This is Skye Fargo," Scarface said. "Some call him the Trailsman. He's not here for the gold." He paused. "For that matter, neither am I."

"Why are you, then?"

"For the blood I can spill."

Stokes shook his head and muttered something and went back to tying.

Fargo felt the rope tighten. He saw that Scarface's rifle was across his lap, the Henry and Colt on the ground beside him. Nash had his hands on his hips. Lucian was drinking. And Stokes was tying him. Not one was holding a gun. There would never be a better chance.

Exploding into motion, Fargo kicked at the fire. Flames and sparks arced at Scarface and the breed threw himself aside to keep from being singed. Spinning, Fargo drove his knee into Stokes's groin, shouldered him out of the way, and bolted. In a few strides he was out of the firelight. As he weaved around a boulder, a shot cracked and the slug whined off it.

Tugging furiously at the rope, Fargo plunged farther into the night. Stokes hadn't had time to tie more than one knot. It only took a few moments to loosen the rope enough to cast it off.

Boots thudded in his wake.

"Which way?" Stokes hollered.

"Over here!" Nash shouted, but he didn't sound anywhere near Fargo.

"Are you sure?" Lucian called.

Fargo wasn't concerned about the three stooges. It was Scarface he was worried about. He ran another twenty or thirty yards and darted behind a stone slab and crouched. Slipping his hand into his boot, he palmed the Arkansas toothpick. It was the only weapon he had left.

The night went quiet.

Fargo stayed where he was. To move invited discovery. After a long while the faintest of scrapes alerted him he wasn't alone.

A shadow moved, a patch of ink darker than the night.

It glided near to the slab, and stopped.

Fargo coiled to strike. Scarface might get him, but he would make damn sure to bury his blade in the breed before he went down.

"Where did he get to?" Nash yelled from a considerable ways off.

"Over here," Stokes answered from not quite as far.

The shadow melted away.

It occurred to Fargo that his rifle and six-gun were probably still by the fire. He could slip in, grab them, and slip out again. Except for one thing: Scarface.

Reluctantly, Fargo turned and worked his way to the Ovaro. He climbed on and reined to the west in a wide loop that, an hour later, had him well ahead of the outlaws.

He used his spurs.

The Pedersons needed to be warned. Dealing with the Apaches was bad enough. Scarface compounded the danger tenfold. Unless they turned around and flew like the wind for Cemetery, they were as good as dead.

Once again their fire was a beacon for every hostile and bad man within miles.

Fargo slowed a couple of hundred yards out. There they were, seated around the fire, easy targets for anyone with a rifle.

Their mounts and packhorse and Mabel were in a string just beyond.

When he was close enough Fargo cupped a hand to his mouth. "Hello, the camp," he hailed them. "I'm coming in. Don't shoot."

Ginny and Carol scrambled up with their Henrys to their shoulders.

Abner stayed where he was, a tin cup cradled in his gnarled hands.

"That you, Fargo?" Ginny called out.

"It's him," Abner said.

Fargo came into the light and drew rein. Before he could get a word out, Ginny took a step and fixed a bead on his chest.

"You have your nerve, you son of a bitch, after what you did to me."

"What are you doin' here?" Carol asked. "How did you find us?"

"Ain't it obvious?" Ginny said. "He must have been shadowin' us. He wants the gold for himself."

"We don't have the gold yet," Carol said. "Why would he show himself until we do?"

"He figures he can disarm us and make Uncle Abner tell him where it is."

"Why don't we let him talk for himself?" Carol said.

"Talk, hell." Ginny's eyes glittered like twin quartz daggers. "He made a mistake comin' in like this. The last mistake he'll ever make." She pressed her cheek to the Henry. "I'm fixin' to shoot this bastard smack between the eyes."

14

"Any last words?" Ginny asked.

Fargo was set to dive from the Ovaro. He'd already slipped his boots from the stirrups. "Just one," he answered. "Scarface."

"That's your last word?" Ginny said.

"Who?" Carol asked.

Abner's head snapped up and his twin eye patches swiveled toward the Ovaro. "What about him, mister?"

"He's following you," Fargo said. "Him and three others. The three were in the saloon in Cemetery and heard you tell the barkeep about the gold."

"The hell you say," Abner said.

Ginny said, "Now you claim someone *else* is after the gold?"

"Hush, gal," Abner said. "This is serious. You're not to shoot him, you hear?"

"I'll do what I damn well please," Ginny replied angrily.

Fargo was ready. He kicked the muzzle of her Henry and vaulted from the saddle and was next to her before she could recover and point it at him. As he had done at the trading post, he did here: he punched her in the gut. And he didn't hold back. The blow folded her in half. Wrenching the Henry from her hands, he trained it on Carol. She made no attempt to raise her own.

"What just happened?" Abner asked.

Ginny sputtered and stumbled with her hands pressed to her belly. "Kill you!" she rasped. "So help me God, I'll kill you for this."

"Hush, I said!" Abner said sternly.

Ginny sank to her knees and groaned.

Carol was grinning. She sat back down and placed her rifle on the ground and picked up her tin cup. "Join us, why don't you, handsome?"

Fargo hunkered where he could watch all three. He held on to the Henry.

"I want to hear about Scarface," Abner said. "How do you know all this?"

Fargo told him. He didn't leave anything out. Not even the embarrassment of having his rifle and pistol taken.

Abner rubbed his chin and then one of his eye patches. "This is bad. This is very bad."

"So you believe him, Uncle?" Carol asked.

"Does he have his Colt?" Abner returned.

Carol glanced at Fargo's holster. "No."

"Does he have his rifle?"

She glanced at the saddle scabbard on the Ovaro and then at her sister's rifle in Fargo's hands. "No."

"Does he strike you as loco?"

"No."

"He'd have to be to ride in here without his hardware," Abner said. "No, he's tellin' the truth, girl, and we're in a heap of trouble."

Ginny had stopped sputtering. "I don't care if he's tellin' the truth or not. I aim to put windows in his skull."

"Like hell you will," Abner said. "Listen to me and listen good. We need his help."

"Like hell we do," Ginny mimicked him. "You have us. What do you need him for?"

"Scarface is about the worst killer on the frontier, next to Red Dog," Abner said. "The things I've heard would curl your toes."

"We're not infants," Ginny said.

"You're no match for him, either," Abner said, and shook his head. "Scarface and Red Dog, both. And me blind. The Almighty must be awful mad at me."

"You're talkin' nonsense," Carol said.

Fargo cleared his throat. "You're safe until you find the gold. Maybe."

"Maybe?" Abner said.

"Scarface might take it into his head to grab your nieces and force you to show him where the gold is, or else."

"Or else what?" Ginny asked.

"Don't be stupid," Abner snapped. He fixed his patches on Fargo. "I am open to ideas. What do you reckon we should do?"

"Trick him. Lure him in. Have him ride into our sights when we're ready for him."

"And how do we go about trickin' someone as canny as he is?"

"You pretend to find the gold."

Abner was still, and then he grinned. "You know, that just might work."

"We ambush him, you're sayin'?" Ginny said.

"Sometimes, girl," Abner said, "you make me wonder if you're really kin of mine."

"Uncle!"

"There is one thing," Fargo mentioned.

"Don't hold back now," Pederson said.

"Scarface will see I'm riding with you. He'll know I told you."

"And he'll be extra suspicious of anything we do," Abner concluded. "We might not be able to trick him, but I reckon we have to try."

"What about the Apaches?" Carol asked.

"We keep our eyes skinned for them as well," Abner said, and chuckled. "Aren't you glad you agreed to help me?"

"I didn't figure on all this," Carol said.

"Who cares about some breed?" Ginny snapped. "Breeds don't scare me no how."

"You are a wonderment," Abner said.

"I'm mad, is what I am." Ginny glowered at Fargo. "But for your sake, Uncle, I'll call a truce with this bastard. Until we deal with Scarface and his pards, that is."

"We might need his help after, too," Abner said.

"You make it sound like we can't do without him."

"Could be we can't."

Carol ran her eyes up and down Fargo's body. "I don't mind that one bit."

"Don't you even think it," Ginny said. "It'd be an insult to me."

"Think what?" Abner asked.

"Never you mind," Carol said.

"I want my rifle back," Ginny demanded, holding out her hand.

"No," Fargo said.

"Damn you, it's mine. You can't just waltz in here and steal it."

"I'm borrowing it."

Ginny reached for the knife in her hip sheath. "I will gut you, so help me."

Abner swore. "For the last damn time, simmer down. If he wants to borrow your Henry, let him."

"Whose kin are you?" Ginny retorted.

Fargo stood and went to the Ovaro and took hold of the reins. "I'll see you in the morning."

"Wait," Abner said. "Where are you goin'?"

"To get some sleep."

"Why not sleep here with us?"

Fargo glanced at Ginny. "I'd like to wake up in the morning." He started to lead the stallion away. "I won't go far. Anything happens, I'll hear."

"Mister?" Abner said.

Fargo stopped.

"I'm obliged for the help. This is twice now you've saved my bacon."

"It's not saved yet," Fargo said. He nodded at Carol and left. True to his promise, he went barely twenty-five yards. At a flat spot flanked by boulders, he stopped and stripped his saddle off and prepared to bed down. He was bone-tired.

Opening his saddlebags, he found his picket pin. In Apache country it wasn't wise to leave a horse loose. He used a rock to pound it in and tied the Ovaro so the stallion faced the Pederson camp. His precautions taken, he stretched out with his back on his saddle and sighed.

As tired as he was, sleep proved elusive. He'd drift off only to snap awake. He didn't know why. He didn't hear anything. Along about the fifth or sixth time, he opened his eyes and the Ovaro was staring into the darkness, its ears up.

Fargo put his hand on the Henry.

A figure ambled toward him out of the darkness. The way it moved told him it wasn't an Apache or Scarface or any of the outlaws.

"What do you want?"

"Is that any way to greet a lady?" Carol Pederson said. Her rifle was across her shoulder, and her other hand was hooked in the front pocket of her britches.

"It's a little late for a visit."

"Not when I had to wait for my uncle and my sis to fall asleep." Carol stepped to the Ovaro and patted it. "Nice animal you've got here."

"I think so."

"About the finest I ever saw, and I know horseflesh." She looked over her shoulder at him. "I know man flesh, too."

"Hell," Fargo said.

"Listen to you," Carol said. "As if you'd turn me down."

"Your sister would throw a fit."

"Ginny does what she likes," Carol said. "I do what I like. I took a shine to you from the start."

"You don't say."

Carol sashayed over and squatted. "You won't be disappointed."

"Brag much?"

Carol laughed. "I'll be as good as Mary McKindrick, I can tell you that."

"What about her?"

"Did you think no one knew? Her husband does. My uncle told me."

"Hell," Fargo said again.

"Abe woke up when she was sneakin' out to pay you a visit. Made him mad as hell."

"He never said anything."

"Yellow curs don't bark at wolves," Carol said. She touched a finger to his chin. "So, what do you say?"

"Now? With Scarface out there? And Red Dog somewhere around?"

"You'd let little things like that stop you?" Carol smiled and made a *tsk-tsk* sound. "And here I thought you had grit."

"Women," Fargo said.

"You like us and you know it. Fact is, my uncle was sayin' as how you have a reputation for pokin' just about every filly you come across."

"There are a few I haven't."

"I don't aim to miss out." Carol gazed off across the mountains. "But I reckon you're right. This ain't the time. Too bad." She rose and cradled her Henry. "A word to the wise before I go."

"I'm listening."

"Ginny is out for blood. She'll stick you with her knife. Bash you with a rock. Anything. You'd better be careful or you'll be dead."

"You're warning me about your own sister?"

"I know," Carol said. "Blood is supposed to be thicker than water. Ain't that the sayin'? But blood is one thing and a good fuck is another." She smiled and winked and strolled away.

"I'll be damned," Fargo said.

15

A pink blush framed the eastern horizon when Fargo stepped into the stirrups and reined toward the Pederson camp.

Their fire had burned to embers. Two forms were still bundled in blankets, but the third was nowhere to be seen.

Fargo had to pass a chest-high boulder. He almost missed the streak of movement. Shifting, he didn't have the Henry quite level when Ginny Pederson sprang. He got a hand up and grabbed her wrist to keep her from burying her knife, and the next moment they tumbled from the Ovaro with her on top.

Fargo hit hard. She hissed and clawed at his eyes and he seized her other wrist. Her own eyes were pools of raging hate. She swore and strained to sink her blade into him. It was all he could do to prevent it. Suddenly she twisted and drove a knee between his legs. Pain burst in waves, and his grip weakened. Not much, but enough that Ginny grinned and put all her weight into forcing the knife into his chest.

Fargo had had enough. He let go of the hand she had tried to claw his eyes with and slammed his fist into her jaw. Once, a second time, a third, each rocking her.

He cocked his fist to do it again, but her eyelids fluttered and she let out a long breath and collapsed on top of him. Tearing the knife from her grasp, he shoved her off.

"Took you long enough."

Fargo sat up.

Carol was leaning on her Henry and smirking. "She almost had you."

"Thanks for lending a hand."

"Crybaby," Carol said. "I won't help her because she's

bein' a lunkhead and I won't help you because if you can't lick a female you're not worth beddin'."

"Next time I might not be able to go so easy on her," Fargo said.

Carol shrugged. "She brought it on her own head. I tried to talk her into leavin' you be, but she's too damn stubborn."

Abner appeared, scratching himself and smacking his lips. "I heard some of that. A hell of a thing to wake up to."

"She keeps this up I'll have to tie her," Fargo warned them.

"Do what you have to," Abner said. "You can't be lookin' out for Scarface and Ginny both."

"I'm glad you see it my way."

"I just don't want to die before I do what I've set out to."

"You and your gold."

"That, too," Abner said.

Fargo stood. He drew his toothpick, cut his rope, and bound Ginny's wrists behind her back. He was finishing the last knot when she stirred and opened her eyes.

"What the hell?"

"Have a nice nap?" Fargo said.

Cursing lustily, Ginny rolled onto her side and twisted her head so she could see her wrists. "You son of a bitch. Get this off."

"No."

"I will by God kill you."

"You aim to kill me anyway."

"Sis? Cut me loose."

"Can't," Carol said.

"Why the hell not?"

"You didn't listen to anything Uncle Abner said last night, did you?"

Ginny turned to Abner. "Uncle? Don't let him do this to me."

"I'm sorry, gal," Abner said.

Ginny swore and got to her knees and turned toward Fargo. "If it's the last thing I ever do, I'll kill you. I swear to God."

"Leave it be," Carol said.

"My own sister," Ginny said. "I'd never let anyone do this to you."

"You'll get us killed if you're not careful."

"Hogwash. I want to live as much as you do."

"I could use some coffee, gals," Abner said.

Fargo could use some, too. His back was sore where he'd hit the ground, and his left elbow pained him when he bent it.

Ginny sat with her body in a bow and her hair falling over her face. "I'll remember this, Uncle."

"I hope so," Abner said. "You never were good at learnin' your lessons."

"I've learned I can't trust my own sister and my own uncle."

Abner sighed.

The sun was up when Fargo was handed a cup. Carol had added sugar, a rare treat.

"I've been thinkin' about your idea," Abner said, "and I've got me a notion how and where. About ten miles north of here is a canyon. It's not long and it's not wide and there's not much cover. We can go on through and out the other end and climb to the top. When Scarface shows, we turn him into a sieve."

"My idea was to pretend you'd found the gold," Fargo reminded him.

"This will work just as well."

Fargo debated. It might, at that. Carol and he could pour down fire from the rim. It would be over before Scarface could rein away. "All right," he said. "We'll give it a try."

"How long are you plannin' to keep me tied?" Ginny asked.

"Until hell freezes over."

Carol laughed.

"Keep pilin' on the insults," Ginny said. "That's the way to win me over."

"I wish you would grow up," Carol said.

"It wasn't you he hit."

"Sis, you're in the wrong on this," Carol said bluntly, "and it could get us killed. Much as I care for you, I care for Uncle Abner and my own hide, too."

"He trusses me like a calf for slaughter and you do nothin'?"

Carol sighed. "I've spoken my piece. I won't say any more. If you'd come to your senses, he wouldn't keep you tied."

"Senses, hell."

Fargo was through trying to reason with her. There were bitches, and then there were bitches. Ginny Pederson was the bitch of the century.

They got under way. Fargo led Mabel and a packhorse. Carol led her uncle and her sister and the other horses.

By the middle of the morning, they were roasting.

Lizards skittered and buzzards wheeled and the breeze was as hot as everything else.

All morning Fargo watched for sign they were being followed, but Scarface was too smart to give himself away. As for the Apaches, if any were around they might as well be invisible.

The heat took a toll on their animals. It was past noon when they reached the canyon. They went in one end and out the other.

Fargo drew rein and dismounted. They allowed themselves some water from a water skin.

Carol held it to Ginny's mouth so Ginny could drink, and when Ginny was done she growled, "Thanks for nothin'."

Her mood didn't improve any when Fargo commenced to bind her ankles.

"What the hell?" Ginny tried to kick him in the face.

Fargo slammed her legs down and put his knee across her shins and went on tying.

"Ain't her wrists enough?" Carol asked.

"You know they're not," Fargo answered. It would be easy for Ginny to get loose with just her wrists tied. "Find me something to gag her with."

"No, you don't," Ginny hissed. "I'll bite your damn fingers off."

"You give us away, we're dead."

"Why would I do that?" Ginny said. "I want *you* planted, not the rest of us. I won't bring harm to my sis or my uncle."

"So you say."

"You know, mister," Ginny said, "I've never hated anyone as much as I hate you."

"I'll try not to lose sleep over it."

"Don't gag me. Please. I give you my word I won't let out a peep."

Abner said, "You can trust her on this, son. She's got a temper, but she likes breathin' as much as we do."

Fargo wasn't so sure. Carol looked at him in silent appeal, and against his better judgment, he grunted and said, "All right. But if she acts up, from here on out she'll be gagged permanent."

"Don't expect me to be grateful," Ginny said.

"The only thing I expect from you," Fargo said, "is to be a bitch."

It took longer than Fargo liked to find a way to the top. They had to do a lot of scrambling up steep inclines and at one point they had to climb a near-vertical but low cliff. Once they gained the rim, they had a clear view of the canyon from end to end.

"Uncle Abner picked a good spot," Carol said. She'd kept up with Fargo with no problem and wasn't breathing hard at all.

Fargo complimented her on it.

"You keep forgettin' I'm a farm girl and not no prissy city gal. I can ride and I can shoot and I've been climbin' trees and such since I was knee high to a calf."

Fargo stretched out on his belly. They were about seventy feet above the canyon floor. An easy shot to make.

"Let's hope Scarface falls for this."

"It'll be like shootin' clay targets," Carol said as she stretched out next to him.

Fargo liked the fact that between their two Henrys, they could pour thirty-two slugs into Scarface and company as quick as anything.

As if she was thinking the same thing, Carol said, "We'll shoot those vermin plumb to bits."

They settled down to wait.

Fargo felt the sun roasting his back. A fly tried to annoy him, but he ignored it.

"You know," Carol said, "if this works out and we don't have to worry about them anymore, tonight would be nice."

"You're forgetting the Apaches."

"To hear you talk, folks in these parts should all be like priests and nuns."

"I'll think about it."

"Care for a peek at my tits to whet your appetite?"

"Now?"

Just then a rider appeared at the far end of the canyon. After him came others.

"Well, damn," Carol said. "I reckon my tits will have to wait. It's killin' time."

16

Fargo started to chuckle at how eager she was, and the sound died in his throat.

Seven riders had filed into the canyon and more were still coming.

"Hold on," Carol said. "I thought you told us it was Scarface and three white men. They all look like Indians to me."

"They are," Fargo confirmed. "They're Apaches."

"What the hell? We have Apaches doggin' us, too?"

"I told you about Red Dog," Fargo reminded her.

"Is he one of them?"

Fargo couldn't tell. The warriors were a long way off yet. When no more entered the canyon, he counted them. "Fourteen."

"We didn't reckon on this."

Fargo debated trying to get out of there before the war party reached the near end of the canyon and decided against it. The old man and the packhorses would slow them down.

"My sis and my uncle will be sittin' ducks if any of those savages get past us."

"Go back down and fan the breeze," Fargo said. "I'll hold the Apaches as long as I can."

"You can't stop that many by your lonesome."

"I can buy you time."

Carol looked at him and her mouth quirked. "Listen to you. You're not as tough as you make yourself out to be."

"You saw what they did to your uncle."

"So? We knew the risk comin' in."

The lead warrior drew rein. Sliding down, he hunkered and examined their tracks.

Fargo recognized him. "Red Dog."

"You don't say." Carol sighted down her rifle. "We shoot him, we'll be famous."

"He's too far off yet."

"I bet I could drop him. But we'll let 'em get closer so they won't have a prayer."

Fargo didn't share her confidence. She didn't have his experience with Apaches.

Red Dog climbed back on his horse. He pumped his arm and the warriors came on at a fast walk.

Fargo noted their rifles. Red Dog had a repeater. So did several others. Repeaters with brass receivers. "Some of them have Henrys, too."

Carol took aim. "Let me shoot Red Dog. I ain't ever been famous before. I bet they write about me in the newspapers and everything."

"I'll fire first," Fargo said. For all her bragging, he hadn't seen her shoot yet.

"If we both shoot him I can't claim credit."

"We can share it," Fargo said. Not that he would ever tell anyone, except to report to the army that Red Dog was dead.

"It wouldn't be the same."

Fargo couldn't believe she was arguing about it; she picked a damn fine time to be temperamental. "You're forgetting the others."

"I'm not forgettin' nothin'. Shootin' them won't make me famous."

"Fame, hell. It's our hides, remember?"

"Fine," Carol said. "We'll do it your way."

"Thank you," Fargo said, to try to stay on her good side.

The Apaches were midway along. They constantly scoured the rims and were poised for fight or flight.

"They suspect somethin'," Carol said.

Fargo ducked and told Carol to do the same. The clomp of hooves grew louder until he judged that the war party was almost directly below. Taking his hat off, he rose high enough to see over.

Red Dog's attention was on their tracks.

Fargo took aim. In a few moments he would have the scourge of the territory dead to rights. He put his thumb on the hammer and his finger on the trigger.

Carol Pederson chose that moment to rear up on her knees and cry out, "Got you, you red devil!" Her Henry boomed.

Fargo could have told her what would happen if she tried something so dumb. And it did.

Red Dog spied her as she was rising and reined around before she fired. Bellowing a warning to his companions, he swung onto the other side of his mount and galloped back down the canyon.

Two warriors with rifles raised them to their shoulders and took aim at Carol.

Lunging, Fargo grabbed her arm and yanked her down beside him. Below, the rifles cracked and lead sizzled the space where she had just been.

"Let go, consarn you," she protested.

Fargo rose to his knees. A lot of the Apaches were prudently fleeing. He centered on one who wasn't and shot him through the heart. Another, with a Sharps, took aim. His own shot was swifter.

Carol joined in, working her level like a madwoman, banging off round after found.

A horse squealed and crashed down. The warrior astride it leaped clear. Turning, he held up an arm and another warrior, flying past, bent and swung him up.

A Chiricahua with a bow was drawing the string to his cheek.

Fargo shot him. He shot another. That made four, but ten were left and they were raising so much dust he didn't have a clear shot.

Carol pumped her lever yet again and squeezed the trigger, but her rifle was empty. "Hell," she said, and commenced to reload.

Hanging by an elbow and a heel, Red Dog stayed on the side of his horse until he was at the far end. In a lithe motion he swung up and looked over his shoulder in their direction.

Fargo would swear the son of a bitch smiled.

The war party galloped out of the canyon.

"Damnation," Carol said in disgust. "All I shot was a horse."

Fargo stared at her.

"What?"

"We have to hurry," Fargo advised, and headed down. He suspected the Apaches would circle the canyon and come after them.

"I'm sorry," Carol said, hustling to keep up. "It all happened faster than I expected it to."

"That's how it is with Apaches." Fargo was concentrating on not slipping in the loose talus.

"Why was it them and not Scarface? Does this mean we have both shadowin' us?"

"Less talk," Fargo said in annoyance.

"You're mad, aren't you? That I spoiled things by jumpin' up like I did?"

"You didn't listen worth a damn."

"I never saw anyone move so quick as that Red Dog," Carol marveled. "Anyone else, I'd have blown out their wick."

"Remember that the next time."

"You think there will be one?"

"After we shot four of their friends? They won't rest until we've paid in blood."

Abner was on his feet, his head cocked, waiting. "Well?" he hollered anxiously when he heard them. "Did you do it? Are Scarface and his pards dead?"

Fargo went to answer, but the dirt cascaded from under his boots and he slid a good thirty feet. Regaining his footing, he descended to the bottom.

Abner approached, groping in front of him. "Well?" he demanded again. "Why didn't you answer me? Did you shoot them dead or not?"

"Not," Fargo said. "It wasn't Scarface."

"Eh?"

"It was Red Dog, Uncle," Carol said.

Abner's face drained of color. "Don't tell me you killed him?"

"We tried," Fargo said, puzzled by the prospector's reaction. "Don't you want him dead after what he did to you?"

"Sure I do," Abner said, bobbing his head. He scratched his chin. "But where did Scarface get to?"

"My guess," Fargo said, "is that he saw the Apaches before they spotted him and he and his friends pulled back."

"Or maybe he skedaddled," Abner said optimistically. "He'd think twice about tanglin' with Red Dog."

Ginny had been listening. "Wonderful," she said. "We have both of them after us now. Can this get any worse?"

Carol was brushing dust from her clothes, and stopped. "It would be nice if we could untie you and give you a gun so you could lend a hand."

"What's stoppin' you?"

"You know damn well. You're liable to put a slug into Fargo here."

"He has one comin'."

"Damn you, sis," Carol said. "It's my life, too. Or don't you care?"

"How dare you?" Ginny said.

"Why can't you call a truce until we have the gold? Give him your word."

"No."

"For me."

"No, I say."

Fargo didn't want to have to watch his back the rest of the way. He had enough to deal with, what with the Apaches and the outlaws. Since appealing to Ginny's common sense hadn't worked, he decided to try something else. "Why did you bother asking her?" he said to Carol. "All your sister cares about is herself."

"What do you know?" Ginny said.

Carol said, "That's not fair."

"But it's true," Fargo persisted. "If she really gave a lick about you and Abner, she would be helping us instead of hindering us."

"Why, you no-account, miserable, stinkin' son of a bitch."

"I love you, too," Fargo taunted.

Ginny flushed with fury. "You wouldn't know the truth if it bit you on the ass. I do so care for my sis, and I'm powerful fond of Uncle Abner."

"Yet there you sit," Fargo said. He shook his head. "The only person you give a damn about is the one you see in the mirror."

"Ask them," Ginny said. "They'll tell you I care."

"Well," Abner said.

"She is how she is," Carol threw in.

Ginny was shocked. "You don't believe I care for you?"

"Not enough, no," Abner said.

Ginny's eyes blazed and she turned to Fargo. "Fine. Untie me. I give you my word that I won't harm so much as a hair on your rotten head until after we have the gold. What do you say to that?"

Fargo bent and drew the toothpick. "About damn time." He hoped he wasn't making a mistake.

17

Fargo had noticed something in his wanderings. Where people had it easy they were soft. Where they had it hard they were hard. And no one had it harder than the Apaches. The land they inhabited was some of the most inhospitable on the continent. Stark mountains, arid plains, little water anywhere. In the summer the land baked and in the winter the cold winds howled.

Small wonder, then, the Apaches were about the hardiest warriors to be found. The Sioux were formidable, yes. The Comanches would fight at the drop of a feather, and they would drop the feather. But the Apaches were tough in a way few others were.

A lot of it had to do with how they lived. They had become one with the hard land they lived in. A warrior could cover more ground on foot in a day than a white man could on a horse. Stealth was their byword. They lived to steal and to kill, and at killing they were masters.

Small wonder Fargo rode with every sense alert, every nerve primed. He had Ginny's Henry across his saddle and a hand always on it. The lead ropes to Mabel and the packhorse were dallied around his saddle horn.

Carol was behind him, leading her uncle. Ginny brought up the rear with the rest of the animals.

"Damn, it's hot," the former complained.

"I've seen it hotter," Fargo said.

"How do they stand it? The savages?"

"They're bred to it."

"I wasn't," Carol said. "But then, when it comes to humid, Missouri has Arizona beat all hollow."

"I wouldn't live here for all the gold in the world," Ginny said. "Look around you. It's a dead land for dead people."

She was wrong about that. There were woods, and some fertile areas. The land had a spectacular raw beauty unlike any other. But all Fargo said was "There are snakes and lizards and Apaches."

"You can keep all three. Once I have my share of the gold, I'm never, ever venturin' west of the Mississippi River again."

"Have plans, do you?" Fargo asked. Not that he cared what she did.

"Damn right I do. Most folks where I come from are dirt poor. I'm goin' to set myself up as a queen and look down my nose at them."

Fargo could see her doing that.

Carol came to her sister's defense, saying, "You've got to understand. Gin and me, a lot of people call us hill trash and treat us like we're no-account." She sighed. "People can be cruel."

"Crueler than animals," Fargo said.

"Ever seen someone mauled by a bear?"

"A bear attacks because it's hungry or to protect its young or defend itself," Fargo said. "People kill other people for the fun of it."

"Well, yes. And people torture other people, where animals don't."

"Cats play with mice."

"And I've seen coyotes play with a rabbit." Carol sighed again. "There are days when this world makes no kind of sense."

They forged steadily deeper into the daunting terrain. Every so often Abner would tell them to look for a certain landmark. He only revealed one at a time. If the sisters caught on that he didn't entirely trust them, they didn't mention it.

By the sun it was about four o'clock when Fargo unwound the lead rope and gave it to Carol. "Keep on riding," he directed.

"Where are you off to?"

"To scout around," Fargo said. "I should be back in an hour."

"What good will it do?"

"It will tell us how close they are."

"Don't get yourself killed," Carol said. "I've taken a bit of a shine to you."

Ginny snorted and declared, "Don't get too attached, sis. When this is over, him and me have a score to settle."

"You could forgive and forget."

"Ha," Ginny spat. "Listen to you. When did you ever turn the other cheek?"

Fargo was tired of her bitterness. He reined away and rode in a wide loop, seeking sign. That he didn't find any was both good and bad. Good, because it meant the Apaches were staying well back. Bad, because he had no idea where they were and they could strike from anywhere at any time.

He rejoined the others.

As twilight was painting the world gray, Abner told them to be on the lookout for gigantic boulders at the base of a rock spire. Presently, they spotted the spire and rode in among the boulders. A small pool of water glistened in the fading light.

"How did you find this water the first time, Uncle?" Carol asked as she was helping him down.

"Girl, I've prospected this country from end to end. I've explored more of it than anyone."

"Except the Apaches," Fargo noted.

They had no fuel for fire, so they ate jerky and drank water and got ready to turn in.

Fargo offered to take the first watch. The sisters would take turns after him.

With a myriad of stars sparkling in the firmament and coyotes wailing, Fargo sat with his back to a boulder and the rifle at his side and probed the night for shadows that moved.

When one did it was by the pool. It rose out of a blanket and came over and sat beside him.

"What do you think you're doing?"

"I can't sleep," Carol said. She smiled and stretched and her breasts pushed against her shirt.

"No," Fargo said.

"I beg your pardon?"

"Not here and not now. I'm not having my throat slit because you want to gush."

Carol laughed. "Listen to you. As if that's why I got up."

"Uh-huh," Fargo said.

She was quiet a while and then said, "Damn you, anyhow. Where's the harm in a quick poke? It'd help me get to sleep."

"You do know we're in Apache country?"

"Keep it up."

"You'd like me, too."

Carol grinned. "You know what? I reckon I'll call your bluff."

"Bluff?" Fargo said. To his considerable surprise, she cupped both her breasts and massaged and squeezed them.

"They're nice and firm," she said huskily.

"No."

Carol pinched a nipple and then the other, and squirmed. "Do that and I get wet."

"You goddamned minx."

Carol unbuttoned her shirt and parted it wide. She was bare underneath, as he'd suspected. Her tits were indeed full and firm, and her nipples rigid. She rimmed her lips with the tip of her tongue. "Like what you see, handsome?"

"I should hit you."

"But you won't." Carol leaned against him, her breath warm on his neck. "About that bluff of yours," she said, and placed her hand on his manhood.

Fargo swore.

"Well, what do we have here?" Carol looked down. "I do declare. I think it's a tree growin'."

"You're enjoying this, aren't you?"

"You say you don't want to, but this pole of yours says you do." Carol rubbed him and cupped him. "Oh my. You keep gettin' bigger. Why is that, do you suppose?"

Fargo was hot all over and randy as hell. Suddenly pulling her to him, he squeezed a breast so hard that she arched her back and gasped.

"Goodness. Rip it off, why don't you?"

"You asked for it," Fargo said, and pushing her onto her back, he tugged at her pants.

Carol grinned and teased him with "Are you fixin' to spank me?"

"Shut the hell up."

"I do so like to be spanked. It makes me squeal and scream."

Only then did Fargo think of Ginny and Abner. They were a good thirty feet away and he couldn't tell if they were awake or not.

"Why did you stop?" Carol looked over. "Oh. Them. Don't pay them no mind. My uncle won't care and my sis won't raise a fuss over a poke, no matter how mad she is at you."

"Some family you have," Fargo said.

"Are you goin' to talk or strip me?"

Fargo stripped her. He got her pants off and pulled his down and pulled her up onto him, her legs straddling his, her nether mount poised.

"Oh my," Carol said in a girlish voice. "You want me to slide down on that huge pole of yours, mister?"

"Bitch," Fargo said, and did the deed himself. Placing his hands on her shoulders, he drove up into her. She stiffened and her mouth parted and he thought she might cry out, but instead she swooped her mouth to his shoulder and sank her teeth into him. Jamming her bottom down, he ground up and in.

"God in heaven, you're good," Carol breathed in his ear. "I knew you would be. A gal can always tell."

To shut her up Fargo twisted both nipples. She shuddered and whimpered and her hot mouth devoured his.

She was good at it; her hips matched his, rhythm for rhythm, thrust for thrust.

Fargo was mad. Not at her, at himself. This was about the stupidest thing he'd ever done. Red Dog was out there somewhere. So was Scarface. Yet here he was, an easy target. His only consolation was that if they shot at him, they'd hit her. The thought made him grin.

"Like it, do you?" Carol whispered. She sank her nails into his arms and bit his neck.

Fargo liked it rough. He bit her and pulled on her hair.

Carol panted and humped faster and cooed, "Yes, yes, yes."

Her uncle and her sister still appeared to be asleep. The horses were dozing and the night was still.

To hell with it, Fargo thought, and let himself go. He rammed her velvet sheath and locked his mouth on hers and felt her jiggling breasts press his chest.

Carol plunged over the precipice first. Her eyes widened and her body broke into spasms of release that ended with her slumped against him, spent.

Then it was his turn. He pressed down on her hips and pumped his own. If the Apaches were to rush them, he was as good as dead. He didn't care. A keg of black powder went off between his legs, and after a while he slumped, too.

Under his breath, Fargo summed it up with "I am one dumb son of a bitch."

18

The next day began ominously.

They were up and had their mounts saddled and Ginny was tying the last pack on Mabel when the quiet cool of the morning was shattered by a piercing shriek. Not a shout or a scream but a shriek of terror that prickled the short hairs at the nape of Fargo's neck. It came from the south, from the direction they had come.

"That's not far off," Abner said, his head tilted.

"Should we go have a look?" Carol asked.

"No," Fargo said.

"But it's a white man," Carol said. "You can tell it's a white man."

"No," Fargo said again.

Ginny's face creased in a sneer. "Is the big brave scout afraid?"

Again the man shrieked. Whoever he was, he was being tortured.

"You should go," Abner said to Fargo.

"Leave you and the women by yourselves?"

Abner nodded. "Might be you can save him like you saved me."

"We'll stay right here," Carol said. "Anyone comes at us, you'll hear me shoot."

"He won't go," Ginny said. "He's got no backbone. All he's good for is hittin' women."

Fargo climbed on the Ovaro and raised the reins. "If I don't make it back, your best bet is to light a shuck for Cemetery."

"And give up on the gold?" Carol said. "Not while we're breathin'."

Fargo frowned and tapped his spurs. He kept his hand on Ginny's Henry.

The dawn was splashing the eastern sky with colors. It lent the land a golden glow that gave the illusion it was as peaceful as Pennsylvania farmland.

Fargo had gone about a quarter of a mile when gibbering and blubbering put the lie to the illusion. He advanced at a walk to a patch of flat ground bare of boulders.

A man had been staked out. As naked as the day he was born, he was red from hair to toes with the blood of a hundred cuts. His toes were gone and his fingers as well, and one other thing, besides. He still had his eyes and they were twin mirrors of a mind on the cusp of madness. He was crying and talking to himself and his body wouldn't stop shuddering.

"It can't be," Fargo said in bewilderment.

Abe McKindrick gave a start at the sound of his voice and blinked and looked wildly about. "Who's there? Is that you? Please, no more. I can't take any more."

Fargo kneed the Ovaro up next to him and leaned down. "It's Fargo," he said, glancing every which way. "What the hell are you doing here?"

McKindrick uttered a strange sort of laugh. "I shouldn't have, should I? But I'd do anything for her. Anything at all. Even try to stop it when I knew I couldn't."

"Stop what? And for who? Mary?"

"She's something, isn't she? A beauty like her with a man like me. I never could get over it." McKindrick shook and groaned. "God, I hurt."

Fargo saw no sign of the Apaches. Climbing down, he held on to the Ovaro's reins, just in case. He hunkered to examine the Apache handwork, and grimaced. The torture had been artfully done. The cuts were deep so they bled a lot, but not so deep they'd be fatal. Not right away. The ground under the trader was soaked crimson and a pool was forming.

"There's nothing you can do," McKindrick said. "There's nothing anyone can do."

"It was Red Dog, wasn't it?"

"How did you know?"

"He was at your trading post to get rifles," Fargo guessed. "He wanted new repeaters and now he has them. I saw him with one."

"You can't blame me."

"I sure as hell can."

"The army investigated me," McKindrick said. "They found no evidence."

"You wouldn't keep a record of it," Fargo said. "You get them on the sly." It was another guess, but he felt it was a good one.

"You resent me for liking to earn a dollar, so you think the worst." McKindrick laughed the kind of laugh ears shouldn't hear. "First her and now this. There's no God, I tell you."

"Confess and I'll let the army know," Fargo said.

McKindrick groaned and raised his head to look down at himself. "They cut off that, too? I didn't even feel it." He grinned hideously. "How can you not feel that?"

"How much did the Apaches give you for the Henrys?"

"Those silly rifles again."

"There's nothing silly about the people the Apaches will shoot with them. It's on your head."

"Me, me, and mine?" McKindrick cackled. "Is this how I'm to be remembered?"

"Why else did you build a trading post in Apache country? Who did you think you were fooling?"

"I fooled myself," McKindrick said sadly, "in so many things."

"How many Henrys did Red Dog get?"

"Sticks and stones. I refuse to be besmirched."

"To be what?"

"You can go to hell, sir," McKindrick said, and passed out.

Fargo got his canteen. He took off his bandanna, soaked it, and applied it to the trader's brow. It was the best he could do. There were too many wounds and the blood loss was too great.

After a while McKindrick coughed and shook and weakly opened his eyes. "I'm still alive?"

"The truth, McKindrick," Fargo tried. "Don't go to your grave with a lie on your lips."

"A lie about what?" The trader seemed genuinely confused.

"The Henrys you've been selling to the Apaches."

"I would never," McKindrick said.

"McKindrick, I saw Red Dog go into your trading post with my own eyes."

"We see but we don't see," McKindrick said, and laughed his mad laugh.

"Do you want me to get word to Mary?" Fargo offered.

"Oh, she'd like that. She's taken quite a shine to you."

Fargo didn't say anything.

"Did you think I didn't know?"

Again Fargo stayed silent.

"Everyone thinks I'm stupid, but I'm not. She does. You do. Abner Pederson does."

"What about him?"

"Don't trust that old coot. Not for a minute. He's the most devious son of a bitch alive." McKindrick coughed and blood flecked his lips. "I should have stayed in Cemetery. But when I saw the dust, I followed. And now look at me." He convulsed, gasped, and died.

"Hell," Fargo said. He didn't know much more than he did before. Rising, he contemplated leaving the body there for the vultures. Instead, he spent ten minutes gathering rocks and covering it.

The stakes the Apaches had used, it turned out, were picket pins they'd probably taken from whites. He put them in his saddlebags.

He roved for sign and found where Red Dog and his warriors had gone off to the west. They wouldn't go far. They weren't about to let prime prey like the Pedersons get away.

Speaking of which, Fargo thought, and he reined to the north.

They were at the pool. Ginny was washing with a cloth. Abner was idly picking at the ground. Carol had her rifle in her hands and she stood as Fargo came around the boulders.

"Aw, damn," Ginny said. "I was hopin' we'd seen the last of you."

"Fargo?" Abner said.

"Who else?" Ginny snapped.

Fargo brought the Ovaro to the water. It was the last drink the stallion would have for a while.

"Well?" Carol prompted. "Are you goin' to keep us in suspense? What did you find?"

Fargo told them about McKindrick.

"Serves him right," Ginny said when he was done. "Sellin' guns to those stinkin' savages."

"I feel sorry for his missus," Carol said. "What will she do now that he's gone?"

Abner was in shock. "God Almighty. And him always actin' so respectable. It goes to show that folks ain't ever as they seem."

Fargo remembered the trader saying the prospector wasn't to be trusted, and wondered why.

"But at least we're shed of Red Dog for a while," Abner went on. "We can strike out straight for the gold and be there by tomorrow night."

"It'll take that long?" Fargo was hoping it would be sooner.

"If it was easy to find, someone else would have found it by now."

"I don't care how long it takes," Ginny said. "Just so we get our shares."

"Niece," Abner said fondly, "there's no two people I care for more for in this world than you and your sister. You came runnin' when I needed you most. I'll never forget that."

"You're kin, Uncle," Carol said, as if that were all the explanation needed.

"My own brother, your pa, wouldn't come. My own sis wouldn't come." Abner shook his head. "No, you two are special to me. You always have been."

"Should I break out a violin?" Fargo said.

"You can be downright nasty at times—do you know that?" Abner said, and stood. "Well, let's fan the breeze. Daylight's a-wastin'."

They didn't fan it so much as plod it. The withering heat took its usual toll and they held their mounts and the pack animals to a walk.

It was the middle of the morning when Carol came up alongside the Ovaro. "My sis is awful mad at me."

"What else is new?" Fargo said.

"She saw that bite mark on your neck and knew what we'd been up to."

Fargo didn't realize he had one. He didn't have a mirror.

"She doesn't like me to fool around with someone she hates."

"No more of that, by the way."

"Say that again?" Carol said.

"Last night I let your body get the better of me. We can't let down our guard like that."

"Listen to you." Carol laughed. "Handsome, all I have to do is put my hand on your cock and you won't be able to keep your hands off me."

The hell of it was, Fargo reflected, she was right.

19

The rest of the day was uneventful. They saw a few snakes. They saw a few lizards. A buzzard circled and lost interest when they didn't drop dead.

The country changed. It became more mountainous with islands of woodland that broke the monotony of stone and dirt.

That night they camped in one of those islands beside a spring of crystal-clear water.

Fargo shot a squirrel and roasted it on a spit over a small fire. Abner and the sisters sat staring at it with the hungry gleam of starved wolves.

Fargo also made coffee. Usually he drank his black, but Abner had a sweet tooth and had brought sugar.

With the stars and the cool breeze and an owl asking the eternal question of its kind, the domain of the Apaches was deceptively peaceful.

When the squirrel meat was done enough, Fargo broke pieces off for everyone. They ate with their hands, the sisters smacking their lips with joy. The hot, juicy meat was delicious.

Fargo was done first. He leaned on his saddle and sipped the sweet coffee and thought about the things Abe McKindrick had said before he died.

Carol finished her portion and wiped her fingers on her britches. "That was right tasty."

Abner nodded with his mouth full. "I do so love squirrel. It's almost as good as painter."

Ginny stopped gnawing on a bone to say, "Shouldn't one of us be keepin' watch?"

"One is," Fargo said, and nodded at the Ovaro.

"You trust that horse with your life?" Ginny said sarcastically.

"Many a time," Fargo said.

"I wouldn't trust no animal no how with mine."

Fargo was tired of her carping. "Keep watch yourself if you want."

"That's all right. I'll take my turn later like we agreed."

Abner sank down with his hands clasped behind his head. His eye patches were incongruously fixed on the heavens as if he could see the thousands of gleaming pinpoints. "Another day and we'll be there."

"Tell me more about this gold," Fargo said. "Is it a vein and you'll have to use a pick and shovel to get it out? Or did you find color in a stream and you'll have to pan for it?"

"I reckon I can tell you that much," Abner said. "It's a vein, all right. About as wide as my arm and pretty near ten feet long."

Ginny whistled.

"That's a heap of gold, Uncle," Carol said excitedly.

"With only the two of you to dig it out, it will take days," Fargo predicted. Wielding a pick was heavy, tiring work.

Abner raised his head. "Hold on. Why only them two? I'm blind but I ain't helpless. I can use a pick, too, if someone tells me where to swing."

"Even with three of you," Fargo said, "it won't be quick."

"What will you be doin' while we're slavin' away in the heat?" Carol asked him.

"Standing guard."

"I'm puzzled by somethin'," Ginny said. "What do you stand to get out of this? It's not like my uncle has cut you in for a share of the gold, like he did us."

"I may get a shot at Red Dog."

"You're goin' through all this just to kill a mangy Injun?" Ginny said.

"There's more," Fargo revealed. "The army asked me to help track down whoever has been selling repeaters to the Apaches."

Abner rose on his elbows. "Do you reckon that's what Abe McKindrick was doin' way out here by his lonesome?"

"Why else?" Ginny said.

Carol picked that moment to stand and say, "I'll be back in a bit." She headed for the woods.

"Where are you goin', girl?" Abner asked.

"Uncle, honestly," Carol said, and shook her head.

"Oh," Abner said.

Fargo drank more coffee and listened to the crackle of the fire. The Henry was at his side, and when the Ovaro raised its head and nickered, he had it in his hands and was on his feet in a twinkling.

"What?" Ginny said.

The stallion was staring in the direction Carol had gone.

"Stay here with your uncle," Fargo said, and ran to the trees. Nothing moved. Warily gliding in among them, he took a gamble and whispered, "Carol?"

She didn't answer.

Fargo went farther. He whispered again. To his right something crashed through the undergrowth. A deer, he thought. He roved back and forth, moving faster. Only when he came to the far end of the woods was he willing to admit the truth.

Abner and Ginny were anxiously waiting, Ginny on her feet and pacing. "No!" she blurted when she saw Fargo emerge alone.

"What is it?" Abner said. "Is Carol hurt?"

"She's not with him, Uncle," Ginny said. To Fargo she said, "Why isn't she?"

Fargo came to the fire and squatted. "Someone took her."

"Who?"

"I won't know until morning."

"Carol is gone?" Abner said aghast. "How did they do it without a tussle?"

"There was probably more than one of them," Fargo imagined.

"She would have put up a fight," Abner said. "She would have hollered to let us know." He stood and shouted, "Carol! Carol! Where are you?"

"Uncle," Ginny said.

"She can't be dead," Abner declared. "I need her. I need the both of you."

"I didn't say she was dead," Fargo said to set him straight. "I said she was taken."

"But what will they do but kill her?" Abner wrung his hands. "And do worse first."

Ginny turned to Fargo. "You're a tracker. Go track her."

"At first light."

"Take a torch," Ginny suggested. "Do it now."

"They'd see me from a mile off," Fargo said. Hell, two miles. "I'd never get close." Or they would lie in ambush and gun him down.

Ginny commenced to pace and to clench and unclench her fists. "My own sister. We've had a few spats lately, but that doesn't mean I don't care for her."

"She can't die on me," Abner said. "I need the both of you."

That made twice the old prospector had said that. Fargo wondered why. "Need her for what?"

"Why, to get the gold out, of course," Abner said.

"You two are forgetting something."

"Oh?" Abner said.

"Whoever took her is still out there and might be watching us."

Ginny stopped pacing. "I hope they try to take me," she blustered. "I'll rip their goddamn eyes out."

Abner put his hands to his eye patches. "Don't count on me for anything. I'm next to useless."

Fargo squatted and upended his tin cup, and the cold coffee spilled to the ground. He refilled it with piping-hot coffee from the pot and took a long swallow.

"How can you be so calm?" Ginny criticized. "I thought you liked her."

"Want me to bawl and pull out my hair?"

About to settle against his saddle, Fargo did the opposite. He set down his cup so quickly he spilled the coffee he'd just poured, and shot to his feet with the Henry trained on two figures who had appeared at the edge of the firelight.

"Don't shoot!" one hollered. "We'd like to come on in and palaver."

"Step out where I can see you," Fargo commanded.

Nash strode into the open, his thumbs hooked in his gun belt. He was grinning. "Squeeze that trigger and you'll never see that pretty gal again."

"Who's that with you?"

Nash motioned, and into the light, showing no fear whatsoever, stepped Scarface. "We meet again, scout," he addressed Fargo.

"Who's that?" Abner said. "Who's there?"

"I'm Nash Rancet and this handsome cuss next to me is called Scarface," Nash declared.

"My God," Abner said. "Is there no end?"

"Think of us as your new best friends," Nash said.

"And we'll stay friendly only so long as you do exactly as we say."

Scarface grunted. "You not do as we say, we kill girl."

Ginny looked ready to tear into him. "You've got my sister? I thought the Apaches did."

"Red Dog rode away after he killed the trader," Scarface said. "I saw him go."

"Where do you have my sister?" Ginny said. "Tell me, you bastard, or so help me, you're worm food."

"Now, now, lady," Nash said. "You lift a finger against us and she stops breathin'. Is that what you want?"

"Tell me, damn you."

"Our pards are keepin' an eye on her," Nash said. "Don't you fret. They won't let anythin' happen to her. She valuable to us."

"He'd not lying about having pards," Fargo mentioned. "There are two others."

"What do you want?" Abner asked.

Now that he had them over a barrel, Nash puffed out his chest. "It's simple, old man. We know about you and the gold. And we aim to swap you for it."

"Swap?" Abner said.

"Have't you figured it out yet? Go on as you are. Find the gold. We'll be keepin' an eye on you, and when you have it, we'll give you the girl and you give the gold to us."

"Never," Ginny said.

"I wasn't talkin' to you, bitch," Nash said. "It's your uncle who has to decide."

"If you do not give us the gold," Scarface said, "the one you call Carol will take a long time to die. A very long time," he stressed.

"Don't you dare hurt her," Abner said. "That girl means the world to me."

"Do we have a deal, then?" Nash asked.

Abner Pederson deflated like a punctured water skin and sadly bowed his head. "We have a deal."

20

"Remember. We'll be watchin' you" were Nash's last words before the pair walked off.

Fargo partly blamed himself. He shouldn't have let Carol go off into the woods alone. He should have insisted Ginny go with her. But then maybe both women would be captives.

Abner was crushed. He sat with his knees to his chest and his arms around his legs.

Ginny, on the other hand, was mad as hell. She cast venomous looks at Fargo and finally boiled over with "Big help you were. You didn't say much and didn't do a damn thing."

"Do you want your sister dead?"

"That's no answer. We could have gotten the drop on them and made a swap of our own. Them for my sis."

"And what if one of the others was off in the trees with a rifle?" Fargo wouldn't put it past Scarface to have thought of that.

"Do you have any kind of plan to get Carol back?"

"Yes."

"Are you goin' to tell me what it is?"

"No."

"Why the hell not?"

"Because you're a bitch," Fargo said. The other reason was that he wasn't sure it would work; he'd wait for daylight, track Scarface and Nash to their camp, settle their hash and save Carol, and all would be well. Or as well as it could be with the Apaches still out there somewhere.

"She was nice to you, mister," Ginny said. "Nicer than you deserved. You owe it to her to bring her back safe."

Abner said, "I shouldn't have brought you gals into this."

"You did us a favor," Ginny said. "We'll be rich if this works out."

"That's just it." Abner buried his eye patches on his knees. "I didn't count on any outlaws gettin' involved. I figured all we'd have to worry about was Apaches."

"We'll beat them both yet," Ginny said. "Wait and see."

The wonder of it was, Fargo realized, she believed that. She was so full of herself, she thought she could get the best of one of the worst renegades on the frontier and an Apache whose string of those he'd killed was longer than her arm.

"I'm not lettin' nothin' keep us from the gold," Ginny vowed.

Abner, at least, was more worried about Carol. "This plan of yours," he said. "You're fixin' to go after them, aren't you?"

"Unless you can come up with something better," Fargo replied.

"I'm sorry I can't go with you. Gin and me will stay right here until you get back."

"Watch out for the Apaches," Fargo said. "Try to stay alive."

The old prospector said a strange thing. "I don't care about that so much anymore."

Abner and Ginny eventually turned in. Abner fell asleep right away, but Ginny lay on her side, glaring at Fargo, for pretty near an hour, before her eyes closed.

"Bitch," Fargo said under his breath. He hoped that Scarface was right about the Apaches having gone off somewhere. Maybe they would stay away long enough for him to get Carol.

Toward the middle of the night he curled up and let himself drift off. He slept so deeply that when he awoke shortly before dawn, as was his habit, he felt refreshed.

He rekindled the fire and put coffee on and was saddled and ready when a golden crown rose above the rim of the world. He nudged Abner and Ginny with his boot and climbed on the Ovaro as they sleepily sat up and scratched and yawned.

"You're on your own until I get back."

"What if they're watchin' us, like you said?" Abner asked.

"It will be just one of them," Fargo figured, "and I'm

banking he'll stay close to you instead of follow me. They can't let anything happen to you or they'll never get their hands on the gold."

"The damned gold," Abner said.

"My sis comes to harm," Ginny said, "I'll be out for blood. Can you guess whose?"

"Careful," Fargo said. "Your sweet disposition is showing." He tapped his spurs and rode to the north until he came to the end of the woods. Reining east, he followed the curve of the trees, studying the ground. On the south side he found what he was looking for: tracks.

If he read them right, one of the outlaws was still in there, spying on their camp.

Leading the Ovaro in a few yards, he tied him off, shucked Ginny's Henry, and commenced his hunt.

Nash made it easy. He was behind a log, asleep.

Drawing the Arkansas toothpick, Fargo eased onto his belly. He left the rifle lying there and snaked forward as silently as the real article.

He had ten feet to go when Nash unexpectedly sat up. Nash yawned and rubbed his eyes and stared toward their camp. Suddenly he stiffened and blurted, "What the hell? Where did he get to?"

Fargo smiled.

Nash sat straighter. A rifle was beside him, but he didn't pick it up.

His body a steel coil set to spring, Fargo closed in. Whenever his quarry moved, he froze.

Nash looked to the east and then to the west, but he never thought to look behind him.

Fargo was almost close enough. He eased onto his knees.

Nash had his elbows on the log. He placed his hand on the rifle.

In two bounds Fargo was on him. He slammed his left boot down on the barrel to keep Nash from raising it, and as Nash turned in surprise, he punched him in the face. The blow knocked Nash across the log. Dazed, Nash clawed for his six-shooter, but before he could unlimber it, Fargo had a knee on his chest and pressed the tip of the toothpick to the outlaw's jugular. "Think again."

Nash blinked a few times and seemed to be collecting his wits. Blood dribbled from a corner of his mouth.

"Hand off the six-gun," Fargo commanded.

Scowling, Nash complied. He went to speak, but Fargo gouged the toothpick deeper.

"When I say you can."

Snatching the revolver, Fargo quickly back-stepped. "Sit up on the log."

Still groggy, Nash did.

"Where do you have her?"

Touching a finger to his split lip, Nash grimaced and said, "Go to hell."

"You'll tell me," Fargo said. "One way or the other."

"I won't talk easy," Nash defied him. "And when the others see what you did to me, they'll take it out on her."

"And lose their chance at the gold?" Fargo shook his head. "I don't think so."

"Scarface will cut her to pieces. He doesn't give a lick about the gold. All he cares about is killin'."

"I'll ask you again. Where is she?"

"And I'll tell you again to go to hell."

Fargo smashed the revolver against Nash's temple and as Nash reeled, he slashed the toothpick across Nash's forehead. Not deep, but it didn't need to be to have blood pour into Nash's eyes.

Nash cried out and fell onto his back. Covering his face, he bawled, "You've blinded me, you son of a bitch." He swiped with his sleeve, and when the truth dawned, he looked up and glared.

"Where is she?" Fargo asked again.

Nash let loose a string of invectives.

"Dumb as a stump," Fargo said, and slammed the revolver against Nash's left knee.

Nash squealed and drew his leg to his chest. He clamped his hands over the knee and swore more luridly than ever.

"Where?" Fargo said.

"You've killed her—you know that? Do you think I'll let her live after—"

Fargo slammed the revolver into the other knee.

Nash commenced to roll back and forth and hiss and spit

in agony. When he eventually subsided, his brow was peppered with sweat and he was pale.

"I can do this all day," Fargo said.

"You miserable, rotten son of a bitch."

"Where?"

Nash licked his lips, and groaned. "About a mile. In a little canyon the breed knew of. We haven't harmed her. As God is my witness."

"I doubt he pays much attention to you."

Nash scowled. "You're not half as funny as you think you are."

"You're going to take me there," Fargo directed. "Do exactly as I say and you get to live."

"It won't work," Nash said. "You don't know Scarface like I do. He'll hear us comin'. Or sense us somehow. No one ever takes him by surprise."

"I want him to hear us."

"Huh?"

"I want him to see us coming."

"Are you hankerin' to die?"

"On your feet," Fargo said. "We'll collect our horses and be on our way."

"I can't walk yet. You damn near busted both my knees."

"You'll walk or we'll see how well you hear without ears."

"What are you? Part Apache?"

"I'm mad," Fargo said.

Muttering and cursing, Nash made it erect. His face was a mess and he wobbled as he tested one leg and then the others. "God, it hurts."

"Poor baby."

Nash took a step and his leg almost buckled. "See?" he said. "I told you."

"You're doing fine." Fargo stuck the revolver under his belt and picked up the outlaw's rifle.

Nash swore. He shook. But he walked.

Fargo retrieved Ginny's Henry and then Nash's bay and led it by the reins to where he had left the Ovaro.

"Climb on your animal," Fargo directed, and helped himself to the rope on Nash's saddle. He drew his Arkansas toothpick.

It took Nash three tries, but he succeeded. Spent from the effort and the pain, he said, "I am plumb tuckered out."

"One twitch and this knife goes in your balls," Fargo warned. He proceeded to tie Nash's wrists and looped the rope tight about the saddle horn. He also tied Nash's boots to the stirrups. Stepping back, he grinned. "Scarface, here we come."

21

From a distance the rope on Nash's wrists and ankles wouldn't be obvious. Nor would the gag Fargo had shoved in Nash's mouth with the warning that if he spat it out, Fargo would shoot him.

Fargo had rigged a rope from the bay to the Ovaro. He rode a few yards behind the bay, his arms behind his back, Nash's Colt in his right hand. To Scarface and the others, it would appear that Nash had tied him and was bringing him to their camp.

Nash kept glancing back. He knew the ruse might work.

"The question you have to ask yourself," Fargo said after about the eighth or ninth time, "is are they worth dying for?"

The "little canyon" was a branch of a larger one, the opening concealed by a bend in the wall. They went around two turns and ahead were trees and a patch of green grass and a lean-to near and, wonder of wonders, a pond.

"I'll be damned," Fargo said. He wondered if even the Apaches knew about this place.

Horses were picketed under the trees. A fire was burning and Lucian and Stokes were drinking coffee. Lucian noticed them first and jumped to his feet.

Fargo didn't see Carol. That worried him. He didn't see Scarface, either. That worried him more.

"Nash?" Lucian hollered. "What in hell are you doin' here? You're supposed to be watchin' that old goat so he doesn't give us the slip."

"You got the jump on that scout?" Stokes called. "That must have took some doin'."

They rose and came around the fire.

"Cat got your tongue?" Lucian yelled. "Why in hell are you back here?"

From under his hat brim Fargo spied Carol on her side in the lean-to. She had been trussed and gagged.

Lucian took several more steps. "I don't like bein' ignored."

Fargo must act. Any moment, they'd notice something was wrong. Raising his head, he said, "I don't suppose you'd like to hand the girl over to me and let us go in peace?"

"Are you loco?" Lucian replied. "Why would we do that?"

"To live longer," Fargo said, and brought the Colt out and around. He shot Lucian and swiveled to shoot Stokes, but Stokes dived to the ground and caught the lead in his shoulder instead of the chest.

Lucian was still on his feet. He drew the pearl-handled Smith & Wesson and he fired as Fargo fired, stumbled back and fired again, fired a third time as Fargo sent a slug crashing through his brain.

Stokes had rolled up onto a knee and was taking careful aim.

Fargo flung himself from the saddle as the outlaw's six-gun boomed. He heard the passage of an angry bee, and replied with the Colt.

Stokes's throat exploded. It jolted him. He got his other hand down to keep from falling, and gritting his teeth, his neck pumping blood, he tried to aim.

Fargo had one pill left in the wheel; it had to count. He shot Stokes square between the eyes.

His ears ringing, Fargo went to reload. He'd forgotten about Nash and was reminded when hooves pounded and he looked up to see the bay bearing down on him. He attempted to leap out of the way, too late. A battering ram plowed into him and smashed him to the earth.

Struggling to stay conscious, Fargo made it to his knees. Another jarring blow whooshed the breath from his lungs and knocked him flat.

Fargo tried to sit up, but his head was spinning. He heard hooves drum and braced himself, but nothing happened.

His head abruptly cleared and he saw the bay racing down the canyon.

Heaving up, Fargo ran to the Ovaro. He gripped the saddle horn and was about to swing up and give chase when his gaze alighted on the lean-to and its occupant. "Damn," he said.

Nash galloped around the bend and was gone.

Carol was trying to speak through the gag and furiously wriggling her fingers.

"Hold on," Fargo said. The toothpick made short shrift of the rope.

The coils had dug so deep, Carol could barely move her arms. Rubbing them, she exclaimed in amazement, "You came for me! You honest to God came for me."

"Why wouldn't I?"

"I thought I was a goner. They were sayin' as how they aimed to kill me once they got their hands on the gold."

"Where's Scarface?" Fargo was scanning the canyon, especially the shadows.

"He rode off about an hour ago," Carol said. "To keep an eye on the Apaches, I heard them say."

Fargo relaxed a little. "Let's get you back to your sis and uncle. But first." He went about the camp, checking saddlebags, poking under blankets. At last he found what he was searching for: his own Colt and his own Henry, wrapped in a bedroll. He checked that the Colt was loaded and twirled it into his holster. The Henry he shoved into his saddle scabbard. He gave Ginny's rifle to Carol.

She had stood and was stomping her legs to restore circulation. "That damn breed tied the ropes so tight, it hurt like hell." She leaned on him, her breasts cushioned on his chest.

"Was it Scarface who jumped you?"

"It wasn't those peckerwoods," Carol said, with a nod at Lucian and Stokes. "I tell you, that breed is a ghost. I didn't hear him, didn't see him. He snuck up behind me and the next I knew he had his hand over my mouth and was carryin' me like I was a rag doll."

"You're lucky to be alive."

"He made that plain," Carol said. "Scarface told me he'd have gutted me and strangled me with my own innards except he needed me to strike a deal with my uncle." She placed her hand on her belly. "And speakin' of my gut, they didn't let me eat or drink since he caught me. Do you reckon I could help myself to some of their coffee and some food before we light a shuck?"

Fargo doubted Nash would return anytime soon. And with Scarface away, it should be safe enough. "If you make it quick."

"I'm so starved, I'd gobble down a rabbit raw."

Carol filled the tin cup Lucian had been using and thirstily gulped.

A chunk of half-burned venison sat on a flat rock. Flies were crawling on it, but that didn't stop her. She shooed the flies away, tore off a piece, and bit into it with relish.

Fargo stood guard while Carol went on eating and making soft sounds of pleasure. She had been at it several minutes when she glanced up, her mouth smeared with juices, and grinned. "Do you know what I'd like for desert?"

The twinkle in her eyes gave Fargo an idea. "Forget it, you little hussy."

"We're alone."

"We don't know for how long." Fargo told himself he had to use *some* common sense on occasion.

Carol bit and chewed and said with her mouth full, "You're no fun."

"Next to your sister I'm a barrel of laughs."

"She's been carpin', has she, about me bein' taken? It's just how she is. Her nature, you might say. It doesn't mean anything."

"It means I have to listen to her bitch."

"Not for much longer. We'll be at the gold soon and dig it out and then we'll go our separate ways."

"Hurry up and eat."

"Goodness. You're actin' like you expect an arrow in the back."

"It could happen," Fargo said.

"You're too high-strung. Look at me. I was carried off and help captive by a bunch of killers and you don't see me bawlin' my brains out like a lot of gals my age would do."

"You do take things in stride," Fargo said by way of praise.

Carol stared at his crotch. "I know what I'd like to take in stride right now."

"No. And that's final."

"We'll see about that later," Carol said with an impish grin.

While she finished eating, Fargo brought the horses over. He threw a saddle on one for her and tied a pack of supplies on the other along with the guns he'd collected from the dead outlaws.

"Helpin' ourselves, are we?" Carol said. "I'd like that fancy Smith and Wesson my own self."

"It's yours," Fargo said. He was watching down the canyon and thought he saw movement. Grabbing his Henry, he wedged it to his shoulder.

"Somethin'?" Carol asked.

"Could be."

"I reckon I'm done, then." She wiped her fingers on her pants and wiped her mouth with her sleeve, and stood.

"This sure is a pretty pistol." She strapped the Smith & Wesson around her waist and patted it.

"Let's go," Fargo said, moving to the Ovaro.

"Are you sure you saw somethin'? I was about to jump you and rip your buckskins off."

Fargo looked at her.

"I can't help it I love to fuck."

His saddle creaking under him, Fargo climbed on. He gave the lead rope to Carol and started out, the Henry across his saddle. It was nice to have his own hardware back.

"What about the bodies?"

"Buzzards have to eat, too."

As they neared the bend, Fargo slowed. He motioned for her to stay put and moved ahead to where he could see the main canyon. The only living creature was a hawk high in the sky. "It's safe," he called out.

Carol was grinning when she joined him. "Right here is as good as anywhere."

"Give it a rest, woman."

"Most gents would be flattered. They say I'm easy on the eyes."

"Not on the ears."

"Ouch. So I'm a nag now, am I? Well, it comes natural. It's the female in my blood."

"From here on out, not a peep," Fargo warned. He gigged the Ovaro. The only sound was the clomp of hooves. He bet himself she wouldn't stay quiet five minutes, and won.

"So, tell me. Do you reckon we've seen the last of Scarface?"

"No."

"And those Apaches are likely to have a try at us, too, ain't they?"

"They sure are."

"Well, hell," Carol said. "This might have been the last chance we'd have for a while and you turned me down. What were you thinkin'?"

"Sometimes I wonder," Fargo said.

22

Abner sobbed and hugged Carol and made a fuss over her, blubbering, "You're back! You're back! Now we can do it. I needed two and not one or we wouldn't stand a prayer."

"How do you mean, Uncle?" Carol asked.

Abner coughed and said, "Two of you can tote out a lot more gold than just one." He bestowed a sloppy kiss on her cheek. "But don't think that's all you are to me. I adore you and your sis, both."

As for Ginny, she gave Carol a quick hug and stepped back and said, "You ought to be more careful when you take a pee."

They saddled their horses and tied the packs on.

Fargo didn't waste a minute in getting under way.

Abner was excited. He mentioned a landmark, a mesa that could be seen from a mile away, and when Fargo spotted it, Abner fidgeted in his saddle and crowed, "We're close! You hear me, nieces, we're close! Keep those rifles of yours handy. We can't let anyone stop us now."

The next landmark was a cliff with a wide cleft at the center that ran from top to bottom.

"It looks as if a giant chopped it with an ax," was how Abner described it.

Not long after, a cliff answering that description appeared out of the heat haze.

"Make right for it," Abner directed. "For the bottom of the cleft."

Fargo had gone a few hundred yards when he glanced at the ground to his right. Reining over, he came to a stop. "What the hell?"

"Trouble?" Carol asked, leading her uncle over.

"Tracks," Fargo said. Lots and lots of them. Tracks of unshod horses coming and going. And they pointed directly at, and away from, the cliff.

Ginny brought the pack animals up. "Injuns, by God. Apaches, you reckon?"

"Who else?" Fargo said.

"Is there a village near here?"

Not that Fargo knew of. Besides which, Apaches didn't live in villages the way she was thinking they did. "You three stay put. I'll scout on ahead."

"No," Abner said.

"Some of these tracks are only a day or so old," Fargo mentioned. It looked to him as if the Apaches came and went frequently. "It's not safe for you and the ladies."

"We're goin' with you," Abner insisted.

"Uncle," Carol said.

"I know what I'm doin', girl," Abner said. "We'll all of us go. And keep your rifles handy, like I told you before."

To sit there and argue was pointless. Fargo reluctantly rode on, his hand on his Henry.

The cliff was sheer except under the cleft. An open slope led up to it.

Abner cackled and rubbed his hands in glee. "Soon, girls! I'm happy as can be. You've made this old man's fondest wish come true."

"We don't have the gold yet," Ginny said.

"There's more to life than bein' rich, niece," Abner replied.

Which struck Fargo as a peculiar thing for him to say, but he had a more pressing concern. The tracks stretched up the slope and into the cleft. He came to another stop and used what was becoming his favorite expression. "What the hell?"

"What is it now?" Abner asked angrily when Carol drew rein.

Fargo told him about the tracks.

"So?"

"So they go *into* that cleft. There could be Apaches in there."

"Again, so what?" Abner said. "My nieces have Henrys. You have a Henry. Between the three of you, you can cut the red devils to ribbons."

"Why fight if we don't have to?" Fargo countered.

"That's just it," Abner said. "Where do you think I found the vein?" He didn't wait for Fargo to answer. "In that cleft, is where."

"You're joshin'," Ginny said.

"I wouldn't josh about a thing like this," Abner said. "Unless you and your sis want to go back empty-handed after all you've been through, we should ride right in and rub out any savages we come across."

"I'm with Uncle," Carol said.

"So am I," Ginny said. "But were there Injuns around when you were in there, Uncle? Did you know we might run into them?"

"As the Almighty is my witness, gal," Abner intoned, "I didn't see hide nor hair of any redskins. Nor any tracks, neither."

Fargo frowned. The old man was lying. Something was wrong here, but he couldn't put his finger on what.

"You can stay where you are if you want," Abner said to him, "but me and the girls are goin' on. Ain't we, girls?"

"Whatever you say, Uncle," Ginny said.

"We've come this far, Uncle," Carol said. "We'll see it through."

The women rode on.

Swearing, Fargo tapped his spurs and trotted past them. Whatever was up there, he'd face it first. At the slope he slowed to a walk and held the Henry ready to shoot.

Up close, the cliff was immense. So was the cleft. Plunged in perpetual shadow, it was an ideal spot for roving Apaches to spend the night when they were passing through.

Fargo reached the opening. So far he hadn't heard a sound or smelled the smoke from a campfire. Warily, he entered, his finger curled around the trigger. As his eyes adjusted he made out a broad flat area covered with more tracks. And in the middle were the charred embers of not one fire but several. At the moment, as the saying went, no one was home.

Ginny was off her horse before anyone and ran in a circle, saying, "Where's the vein, Uncle? Where's the vein?"

Carol halted and climbed down. She helped her uncle off

and steadied him as he stretched his legs and turned his sight-less eyes on the high walls. "Where do we look?" she asked.

"Not yet," Abner said.

Fargo was the only one who'd had the presence of mind to keep an eye on the entrance, but now he turned and gave the old prospector the same look of surprise the women were giving him.

"You told us the gold was here," Ginny said.

"And it is." Abner bobbed his chin. "But Fargo was right to worry about those tracks. We better deal with the redskins before we set to diggin'."

"At least show us the vein," Carol said.

Abner shook his head. "Not yet, I say. The Injuns could show up at any time. We have to be ready."

The sisters swapped confused glances, and Fargo didn't blame them. "I'll watch for the Apaches while you show them the vein," he offered.

Abner frowned. "Don't any of you have ears? No and no."

"But, Uncle—" Carol said.

Abner silenced her with a chop of his hand. "Listen to me. Look at these patches I'm wearin'. Do you think I want the same thing or worse to happen to you? You want the gold, and I don't blame you. But it's no use to you if you're dead."

"Just one look," Ginny said. "We've come so far."

"Who are you tryin' to fool? You'll want more than a look. You'll take a pick to it so you can hold a nugget in your hand and then you'll want another piece and another. No, I say. We kill the Apaches so we can dig without havin' to worry."

"I suppose that's best," Ginny said, although she sounded as if it was anything but.

"Of course it is. You can't fight Injuns if all you're thinkin' about is the gold."

"I'm thinkin' about it anyway," Carol said.

"Fargo?" Abner said, turning his head from side to side as if he was trying to pinpoint where Fargo was. "Talk to them. Tell them I'm right. We can't breathe easy until the Apaches who use this as a hideout are bucked out in gore."

"Who would these Apaches be?" Fargo asked as he swung down from the Ovaro.

"Eh?"

"The warriors who come here," Fargo said. "They wouldn't happen to be Red Dog's band, would they?"

Abner shrugged. "How would I know?"

"I'm not stupid," Fargo said.

Carol picked up on it sooner than Ginny. "What are you sayin'?"

"You don't find it strange the gold just happens to be at a place Red Dog uses for a camp now and then?"

"Gold can be anywhere," Carol said.

"So this is just coincidence?" Fargo said. "And how is it your uncle snuck in here to look for gold, anyway? Knowing Red Dog might be here?"

Abner quickly said, "I spied on him. I saw him ride off."

"But why *here*?" Fargo said, and motioned at the cleft. "When you had all of Arizona Territory to choose from?"

Ginny cradled her Henry, her brow puckering. "That's a good question."

"Why not here?" Abner said. "I've been grubbin' for gold since before any of you were born. And I found some once in a cleft just like this."

"Imagine that," Fargo said.

"You don't believe him?" Carol asked.

"Those Henrys of yours," Fargo said. "Didn't you say your uncle bought them for you?"

Carol nodded. "So we could look out for ourselves when we came out to be with him. It was right kind, don't you think?"

"He could have bought any rifle."

"But these are the newest and the best," Carol said, patting hers. "Folks are always sayin' how you can load a Henry on Sunday and shoot it all week."

"Or cut loose on Apaches armed with single-shot rifles and they wouldn't stand a prayer."

Ginny walked over. "You're suggestin' our uncle bought these rifles for us knowin' we've have to tangle with them?"

"He not only knew you might, but he led you right to them," Fargo said.

"That's loco," Abner said.

"Prove it."

"How?"

"Show them the gold," Fargo said.

"I already explained why that's a bad idea."

"Uncle," Ginny said.

"Uncle, please," Carol said.

Abner glared at Fargo. "Damn you, anyhow. Why couldn't you keep your mouth shut?"

Carol put her hand on his arm. "It won't hurt to show us."

"I'd like to." Abner sighed. "But the truth of it is, there ain't any."

23

For all of half a minute Carol and Ginny were rooted in shock. Then Carol swayed and put a hand to her throat and said, "God in heaven, no. You wouldn't, Uncle. Tell us you wouldn't."

Ginny refused to accept the evidence of her own ears. "How can you say there ain't any gold?"

"It's pretty easy. Read my lips," Abner said. "There ain't any gold."

"You're funnin' us," Ginny said. "You asked us to come to this godforsaken country to help you pack it out."

"I lied."

"You paid for our fare. You bought us new rifles. You outfitted us with horses and supplies. You wouldn't do that if there wasn't any gold."

"Damn it, girl. Use your ears."

"You did this to your own kin?" Carol said.

Ginny turned to her. "What is he sayin', sis? It can't be true, right?"

"I'm afraid so."

"But there *has* to be gold. Why else did he invite us out here?"

"I'd like to hear that myself," Carol said to her uncle. "Why *did* you?"

"It would only make you mad," Abner said.

Carol clenched a fist. "Do you have any idea how mad *I* already am? You tricked us. You used us. Thanks to you I was taken captive—"

Abner said, "That last ain't my fault."

"We wouldn't be here if you hadn't asked us to come," Carol said.

"Hold on," Ginny interrupted. "I want to be clear. There's no gold? None at all?"

"If your wits were any slower," Abner said, "you'd have been born a tree stump."

Ginny started to laugh, abruptly stopped, then laughed some more, a high-pitched, near-hysterical peal of mirth that ended with her virtually screaming, *"There isn't any fuckin' gold?"*

Before anyone could think to stop her, Ginny sprang at her uncle. She dropped her rifle and grabbed him by the front of his shirt and shook him as a terrier might shake a rat. He cried out and tried to wrest free. Carol leaped to his aid and Ginny pushed her away. *"No gold?"* Ginny screamed. *"No damn gold? No damn gold at all? No gold anywhere?"* And with each shout she shook him harder. Finally she let go and he fell onto his back and raised an arm protectively over his face. She stood over him quaking with tears streaming down her cheek. "No *fuckin'* gold?" she said softly.

Carol put an arm around her sister's shoulders. "I know," she said.

"We were fools," Ginny said.

"I know," Carol said again.

"He's killed us."

"We're not dead yet."

Blinking away tears, Ginny looked at Fargo. "Get us out of here. Take us out now and get us back safe to Cemetery."

"I'll do the best I can," Fargo promised.

Ginny stared at Abner. "Why? Tell me that, you son of a bitch? Why, after we've been so close all these years? Why would you do this to us?"

Abner lowered his arm. His features stricken, he said plaintively, "You were the only ones I could count on to come."

"That doesn't answer the damn question."

"It's that Apache who blinded you, ain't it?" Carol said. "Red Dog."

"What?" Ginny said.

Abner nodded. He slowly sat up and draped his forearms over his knees and bowed his head. "It's why I bought you the Henry rifles."

"What?" Ginny said again.

Fargo wanted to hear this, too, and moved closer. He'd had an insight of his own. "When I saved you from him, you lied to me. Red Dog didn't jump you right when you'd found some gold. He caught you spying on him." He gestured at the cleft. "Spying on him here."

Abner nodded. "This is one of his hideouts. I stumbled on it while I was prospectin'. I was lyin' out there, just watchin', mind you, when some of his bucks came back from huntin' and spotted me."

"From the very start everything has been a lie," Carol said bitterly.

"I haven't lied about carin' for you girls."

"Get to why you sent for us," Ginny snapped.

"That's easy," Abner said, and tapped his eye patches. "It's these."

"I still don't savvy," Ginny said.

"Red Dog took my eyes," Abner said fiercely. "The red bastard gouged them out with his knife and laughed as he did it. My eyes!" Abner roared. "Do you think I'd let a thing like that pass? Do you think I'd turn the other cheek and go on with my life?" He pounded the ground. "No, by God! That son of a bitch deserves to die. You hear me? The Good Book says an eye for an eye. Well, I say a life for my two eyes. His life. I sent for you two, bought you those Henrys so that you can kill Red Dog for me."

"Oh, Uncle," Carol said.

"Don't 'Oh, Uncle' me," Abner said. "You're not blind. Your life ain't ruined. You don't have to give up the thing you love most in the world because some red heathen took your sight away."

"So all this is about you takin' revenge?" Ginny said.

"Can you blame me? After what he did? I can't kill him myself. But you two are crack shots."

Carol's face twisted in disgust. "And to think I loved you so much."

"Don't take that tone with me," Abner said. "You'd do the same if you were in my boots."

"No, Uncle," Carol said. "I wouldn't. I'd never put two people I cared for in danger of losin' their lives to the likes of Apaches."

"We can do it, I tell you," Abner said. "All we have to do is hide and wait for Red Dog and his bunch to show up and pick them off like clay targets at the county fair."

"We?" Ginny said.

"I'm here, ain't I?" Abner said. "I'm next to helpless, but I'm willin' to risk my hide the same as you're riskin' yours."

"That's just it, Uncle," Carol said. "You put us at risk without once askin' how we felt about it or warnin' us what you were up to."

"You're a bastard," Ginny said in scorn.

Abner fixed his eye patches in her direction and then in Carol's. "Here I reckoned you two cared. If you do, if you really and truly do, you'll want revenge on Red Dog as much as me."

Carol turned and walked away, her arms folded across her chest.

Ginny swore and went over to her horse and leaned her forehead against it.

Abner raised his head. "Fargo? You still here?"

"Where the hell else would I be?"

"You savvy, don't you? An hombre like you? A man who never takes guff off anyone?"

"Pederson," Fargo said, and stopped.

"What?"

"Never mind." Fargo walked to the entrance. With all their talk they'd neglected to keep an eye out. He looked and said, "If we didn't have bad luck we wouldn't have any luck at all."

A long line of Apaches, riding in single file, were bound for the cliff. They were coming from the west and were a quarter of a mile out.

Fargo called to the sisters. Carol hurried over, and cursed. Ginny took her sweet time; he had to grab her hand and pull her down. "Let them see you, why don't you?"

"There are a lot of them," Carol said.

"Red Dog, you reckon?" Ginny asked.

"Odds are," Fargo said. "We can light a shuck but they'll see us."

"And with our uncle to slow us down, they'll catch us," Carol said.

"Leave him." From Ginny. "Let them have him."

"They'll finish what they started," Carol said.

"It's what he deserves for trickin' us. The three of us have good horses. We can get away."

"I can't just abandon him," Carol said. "It's not in me."

Ginny was incredulous. "After what he's done?"

"He's our uncle. Don't you remember the good times we had with him when we were little? How he bounced us on his knee and told stories? How he bought us licorice and that jar of hard candy?"

"Candy ain't worth dyin' over."

Carol turned to Fargo. "What about you? Where do you stand?"

"If you stay, I stay."

"True love," Ginny said, and laughed.

"There's only the one way in or out," Fargo said. "And only a few can get at us at a time."

"There are too damn many," Ginny said. "You know there are too damn many."

"With our two Henrys we can spray lead like it was hail," Fargo said to Carol.

Carol looked at her sister. "With three Henrys we can spray more."

Ginny glared at Fargo. "You might fool my sis, but you don't fool me. You've been sayin' all this time about how deadly Apaches are. About how tricky they can be. About how most whites don't stand a prayer against them."

"We can drop a lot of them before they get close," Fargo said.

"We might drop four or five," Ginny predicted, "but that will leave plenty."

"There's no cover out there," Carol said. "We can pick more than that off."

"Listen to you," Ginny said. "The great Injun fighter."

"I'm stayin' and that's final."

"Well, I'm not." Ginny wheeled and strode to her mount and went to climb on. She glanced at Abner, who still sat on the ground with his head in his hands, and then at Fargo and Carol at the entrance. Shaking a fist at the patch of sky visible above the cleft, she shouted, "Damn you to hell." Then she came stomping back.

"Thank you," Carol said.

"Go to hell."

"I'm obliged for your help," Fargo said.

"You can go to hell, too. And I ain't doin' this for you. I'm doin' it for my sis." Ginny stared at the approaching Apaches. "This plan of yours to make a stand. You reckon we'll come out on top because we have repeaters. Isn't that the general idea?"

"That's the idea," Fargo said.

"Well, do me a favor," Ginny said. "Take a gander at that Apache out in front and a couple of the others behind him. Is it me, or are their rifles as shiny and bright as our Henrys?"

"A few of them have repeaters, too," Fargo said. He'd seen them at the canyon.

"Wonderful," Ginny said. "This stand of ours is liable to be our last."

24

Fargo kept silent. Ginny was right. Red Dog and at least two others had Henrys. So their edge was no edge at all.

"Any more brainstorms?" Ginny asked sarcastically.

"Just one," Fargo said. "When we open fire, each of us drops a warrior with a repeater."

"Provided we don't miss," Ginny said.

"You and your sister are supposed to be crack shots."

"With squirrels and such," Ginny said.

"We'll do our best," Carol said. "It's our lives at stake."

"We'd have a better chance if they don't know we're in here," Ginny said.

Fargo knew what she was thinking about: their tracks.

The warriors were coming from a different direction, but when they reached the bottom of the slope, they couldn't help noticing that shod horses had gone up it since they left.

"Too bad there's not some way we could get them to sit still for us," Ginny said. "Then we could pick them off easy as pie."

"I'll go for Red Dog," Fargo said. "Carol, you take the next warrior after him with a Henry. Ginny, the one after that."

"Oh, sure, have me shoot at the one who is farthest away."

"Stop pickin' on him," Carol said. "How was he to know they'd have Henrys?"

Fargo felt a twinge of conscience. He had seen that Red Dog had one at the canyon and hadn't said anything. He still didn't understand why Red Dog had killed McKindrick after the trader went and sold him the new rifles.

"The red devils are gettin' close," Carol commented.

None of them had heard Abner come up and Ginny

jumped when he cleared his throat. "Are you sure you can kill Red Dog with your first shot?"

Fargo knew he was talking to him. "I'm sure as hell going to try."

"I'd like to help."

"You've done enough, Uncle, dear," Ginny said. "Go stay with the horses until it's over."

"Blind or not blind," Abner said, "you don't get to tell me what to do."

"It's for your own good," Carol said. "We can't fight the Apaches and watch out for you, both."

"Who's watchin' out for him?" Ginny said.

"I reckon I deserve that," Abner said. "But I've only ever wanted what's good for you girls."

"Say that lie again," Ginny said, "and I will bash your teeth in."

"Gin," Carol said.

"Well, I will. He's lied to us and used us and then has the gall to say it's been for our own good."

"You sure can hold a grudge," Abner declared.

"Says the man who went to all this trouble to get revenge on the one who blinded him."

"Damn it," Abner said. "You'd have done the same."

"No, Uncle," Ginny said. "I wouldn't."

"Enough," Fargo said. The Chiricahuas were almost to the slope. He centered his sights on Red Dog's chest. They needed to be a little nearer for him to be certain.

Abner didn't heed. "There's not much time, but I'll say my piece anyhow. Ginny, Carol, I love you gals. Love you more than all my other kin put together. You've always treated me decent and I appreciate that. Ginny, you're mad at me right now and I don't blame you. But you don't know what it's like to have your sight taken. To have someone dig a knife into your sockets and rip out your eyeballs. It did somethin' to me deep down inside. It twisted me. It's made me want to kill him more than I've ever wanted anythin' my whole life long. Even if in killin' him I meet my Maker. Try to remember that, later. Maybe you'll think better of me."

"It will be a cold day in hell," Ginny said, "when I think better of you."

"I'm not as mad as she is, Uncle," Carol said. "I'm sad more than mad that you'd do this to us."

"I'm sorry, Carol, gal. The last thing I want is to hurt your feelin's."

"You sure have a damn strange way of showin' it," Ginny said.

"No more talk," Fargo commanded.

The war party had reached the slope. Red Dog started up but immediately drew rein and raised his arm to halt the rest. Bending low, he stared at the ground, then snapped his head up and studied the entrance.

Fargo curled his finger around the trigger. The moment had come.

Red Dog straightened and pointed and said something to the others. Their faces registered surprise.

"Have they seen us?" Carol wondered.

Fargo caught movement out of the corner of his eye. He looked, and swore, and went to stand but caught himself.

Abner had slipped around them while they were concentrating on the Apaches. He had moved along the bluff eight or ten feet and now he was descending the slope, his arms out in front of him, groping the air and grinning like a lunatic.

"Uncle!" Carol breathed, and put her hands flat to push to her feet.

"No," Fargo said, grabbing her.

Ginny laughed. "Let the old fool get himself killed. Who cares?"

Abner shouted, "That's right, Red Dog. It's me! I came back to settle accounts! I know you're down there, you mangy bastard. Speak up. Or are you yellow?"

"What does he think he's doin'?" Ginny said.

Red Dog seemed as stupefied as they were. One of the other warriors gigged his mount up and took aim with a Sharps but Red Dog said something and the warrior lowered it.

Abner continued to descend, stumbling now and again, talking all the while. "I bet you never figured to see me again, did you? Thought you could blind me and that'd be the end of it. Well, guess what, you bastard. I've come back for you. That's right. I'm challengin' you. You and me in a fight to the death. Just the two of us. If you're man enough, that is. Or do you only like 'em tied down and helpless?"

Red Dog glanced at the entrance and at the shod tracks.

Fargo could guess what he was thinking: that Abner hadn't come alone, that there had to be other whites in the cleft.

"Cat got your tongue?" Abner hollered, and stopped. He was about halfway down, and an easy target for Apache rifles. He spread his arms wide. "Here I am. Prove you're man enough. Come up here and kill me if you can."

"The jackass," Ginny said.

"Don't you get it?" Carol snapped. "He's tryin' to draw Red Dog into our sights so we can't miss. He's riskin' his own life to help us."

"I'd admire it more," Ginny said, "if he hadn't tricked us into comin' here."

"*Still* nothin' to say?" Abner called mockingly. "I reckon you're not the holy terror folks make you out to be. You're nothin' but a yellow dog coward."

Red Dog slid from his mount. He spoke and motioned and the other warriors came to the bottom of the slope and stopped. Red Dog said more, then started up on foot, his Henry cradled in his arms.

"Will you look at that?" Ginny said.

"He's playin' right into our uncle's hands," Carol said.

Was he? Fargo wondered. The other Apaches were watching the cleft, not Abner.

Red Dog was grinning like the proverbial cat about to pounce on a canary. "Old white-eye," he called up, and laughed a vicious laugh. "Or maybe should call you old no-eyes."

Abner put his hand on the knife at his hip. "Come and try me, you son of a bitch."

Climbing slowly, glancing repeatedly at the cleft, Red Dog said, "You think you clever, old one. You think me dumb."

"You deserve to die however it takes."

Red Dog motioned again and the rest of the warriors climbed down.

"Uh-oh," Ginny said.

"You try bluff, old one," Red Dog said. "But Shis-Inday not foolish."

Fargo kept his bead on Red Dog. Without their leader the rest might scatter.

"What are you waitin' for?" Abner hollered. Not at Red Dog, but for them to act.

Jerking his rifle to his shoulder, Red Dog bawled in his tongue, "Kill them all!"

Fargo fired, but just as he squeezed, Red Dog dived. He worked the lever and took another bead. Beside him the women opened up, their Henrys banging in unison.

Yipping like wolves, the Apaches bounded up the slope. They stayed low and spread out as they came. Their rifles cracked and thundered, belching gun smoke.

And through it all, Abner Pederson stood with his arms outspread.

Fargo lost sight of Red Dog. He aimed at another. The Henry bucked, the warrior fell. The sisters were firing as fast as they could. Six or seven Apaches were down but it was nowhere near enough.

Red Dog heaved up, squeezed off a shot, and dropped again.

Fargo spotted a warrior with a Henry. He aimed, but Carol's rifle banged first and hair and brains showered from the top of the warrior's skull.

Slugs kicked up dirt practically under their noses.

Arrows whizzed overhead, sometimes missing them by inches.

Suddenly Ginny cried out and clutched her shoulder. She dropped her rifle, her face twisted in pain. "I'm hit bad."

By now the Apaches were more than halfway and climbing with the alacrity of mountain goats. They paid no attention to Abner Pederson.

Blood sprayed from between Ginny's fingers. She slid back, gripping her rifle by the barrel. Carol stopped shooting to help her.

"Hunt cover!" Fargo shouted. They couldn't hold the opening; there were too many Apaches. He fired, worked the lever, fired. He'd thought that all the warriors with Henrys were down except Red Dog, but either he was mistaken or another warrior had helped himself to the Henry of a fallen companion because suddenly a burly Apache hurtled out of the cloud of smoke, letting off shot after shot after shot.

Fargo blasted him. He shot a bowman. He shot a Chiricahua with a Sharps. But he could only do so much. The withering storm of lead and arrows forced him to scramble back or be riddled. Rising to his knees, he reloaded, his fingers flying.

They were about to be overrun.

25

Fargo had long imagined that when his time came he wouldn't die in bed. A peaceful death was for store clerks and bank tellers and those who preferred their lives to be as timid as they were. That wasn't for him. He'd rather go out like this: fighting to the last. Some might say that was childish. For him, it was the result of living his life on the raw edge. In the wilds a peaceful death was rare.

So as he frantically slid cartridge after cartridge into the Henry's magazine, he braced for the end.

Outside, the Apaches whooped and converged. Red Dog shouted in their tongue, "Slay all of them! Do not let one white-eye live!"

Fargo finished and looked up just as two warriors appeared in the cleft. He started to raise his Henry.

On either side of him rifles *spanged*. Carol was on his right, Ginny on his left.

"We're in this to the end," Carol said grimly.

"We die together, sis," Ginny said.

To a chorus of piercing war whoops, Apaches swarmed in the opening. Some let fly with arrows and lead while others drew knives and tomahawks.

Fargo fired, backed up a step as an arrow streaked past, fired again.

"Kill the red vermin!" Ginny shouted.

The three Henry repeaters lived up to their name. They sprayed slugs fast and furious, a withering firestorm of death.

More warriors poured in.

The sisters were shooting, shooting, shooting.

Ginny grunted and rocked on her heels and went back to firing like a madwoman.

Carol staggered. She'd been clipped, but she gritted her teeth and fought on.

So far, Fargo was unscathed. It was a miracle, and it couldn't last forever. He didn't care. He fired, fired, fired.

An Apache with a bow took one in the chest while in the act of drawing the string.

The entrance was filled with bodies.

The wave was lessening.

Fargo felt a stinging pain in his side. He ignored it, pumped the lever, fired. There were so many. He tried not to think of that. He fired. A warrior grabbed his throat and pitched forward. Fargo fired.

The Apaches trying to get in were stepping on the bodies of those who already had tried.

Beside Fargo a rifle boomed. He added his own. Shot after shot until he worked the lever and squeezed the trigger and the hammer clicked.

Only then did Fargo realize all the Apaches were down. He blinked and coughed and swatted at the gun smoke and drew his Colt rather than reload. "We did it," he said in disbelief.

Several of the Apaches still moved. A few were convulsing. They had bullet holes in their heads, in their throats, in their chests and shoulders. Blood flowed in rivulets and spouted like whale holes.

"Where's Red Dog?" Fargo didn't see him. He took a step and it hit him that the women hadn't replied.

Ginny was on her back, her arms outflung, a hole in the center of her forehead, another in her chest, and the one in her shoulder. Her eyes were wide with her hate of everything red.

Fargo turned. "No," he said.

Carol was on her side, her back to him. Blood smeared her temple and there was red on her shirt.

Quickly kneeling, Fargo carefully rolled her over.

Her eyes fluttered and she looked at him and smiled weakly. "Sorry about this. I couldn't dodge 'em all, handsome."

"Don't talk." Fargo pried at her shirt. "Let me see how bad it was." He got the shirt up and his throat constricted.

"I don't need to see," Carol said. She reached up and touched his cheek. "A hell of a note, goin' out like this. We never did get to wrestle naked like I wanted." She grinned.

Fargo glanced at the opening. None of the Apaches were moving.

"Did we get the whole bunch?"

"Appears so," Fargo said, although he had yet to see sign of Red Dog.

"Tell my uncle—" Carol said, and coughed. "Tell him I don't hold it against him. Tell him that to me he'll always be the same uncle who bounced me on his knee when I was a young-un. Tell him—" She stopped and sucked in a breath. "He sure bluffed us good," she said, and went limp.

"Hell," Fargo said. He laid her down and closed her eyes and stood. He was suddenly hot all over, like a volcano about to explode. He went to the opening, stepping over Apaches right and left.

The slope was littered, too.

He found Abner where Abner had been standing when the fight started. The prospector lay in a spreading scarlet pool. His mouth was opening and closing, but no sounds came out and no sound ever would. His throat had been slit from ear to ear.

Hundreds of yards out, a lone rider raised a cloud of dust.

Fargo was tempted to run to the Ovaro and give chase. But he owed it to the women—to Carol, at least—to see that they were buried. And the fleeing rider was leaving plenty of tracks.

He gathered up all the fallen rifles first. There were the two Henrys that belonged to the sisters, and two others he took from dead Apaches. He wrapped them in a blanket and tied them on Mabel.

He used a pick to dig shallow graves for Abner and Ginny. He didn't care if scavengers got to their bodies or not. He dug a deeper grave for Carol, a proper grave, and placed her on a blanket with her arms folded. He had no words. He simply covered her and tamped down the dirt.

The Apaches he left where they had dropped.

He collected the horses that hadn't run off and added them to the string. Then, tired and dusty and simmering with wrath, he took up the pursuit.

The tracks were plain enough. A greenhorn could follow them, and he was no greenhorn.

The sun baked him, but he didn't care. He pulled his hat brim low against the glare. He was a turtle and the other was a hare, but the hare would stop eventually. He didn't care how far he had to go. He wasn't giving up this side of his own grave.

It took forever for the afternoon to give way to twilight. He rode until it was too dark to see the tracks.

Dismounting, he made a cold camp and chewed jerky from his saddlebag. He didn't have much of an appetite. He lay against his saddle with a blanket to his chest and stared at the stars until his eyelids were leaden.

Dawn found him in the saddle and on the move. His quarry was making a beeline to the southeast.

By noon he still hadn't caught up. He stopped and let the Ovaro and the other horses rest for half an hour and was in the saddle again, as determined as ever to see it through.

He thought about all that had happened and if there was anything he could have done differently, and nipped that in the mental bud. The answer was no. It was always no. He wouldn't be a martyr to his mistakes. You made the best decisions you could and got on with your life.

Toward the evening of the second day, the tracks brought him to a maze of interconnected canyons. Without the tracks he would never have found which way the rider went. Up one canyon and down another. It gave the impression the rider was wandering aimlessly, but he suspected otherwise.

The smell of wood smoke proved him right.

Fargo drew rein and alighted. He ground-hitched the Ovaro and coiled the lead rope around a boulder. Yanking his Henry from the scabbard, he crept forward.

From around the next bend came voices.

He flattened and crawled and took off his hat before he looked. He supposed he shouldn't be surprised, but he was.

There were three of them. They were seated around the

fire, the half-breed and the white man drinking coffee, the Apache cross-legged with his hands on his legs.

Fargo could try to drop them where they sat, but the breed and the Apache were quick enough that they might make it to cover. He decided to wait.

Full dark descended.

He caught snatches of talk. Some of it was about him.

Some of it was how Red Dog planned to drive the whites from Apache country.

Their fire was small. The light barely reached out ten feet. He felt safe in crawling along the canyon wall until he was close enough that he could have tossed a pebble and hit one of them.

Nash was speaking. " . . . can keep on like we have been. I'll find a couple of hombres to take Lucian's and Stokes's place."

Scarface said, "Maybe I will find two friends instead. Your friends die too easy."

"Against most they were good enough. That Fargo ain't like most."

Red Dog grunted. "Him not kill easy. Only white man good as Apache."

"Thanks," Nash said.

"Scarface right," Red Dog said. "Most whites die easy. Apache kill them, it like kill babies. Not Fargo. Try to kill him like try to kill Apache."

"What will you do with your band wiped out?" Nash asked.

"Same as you," Red Dog said. "Find more warriors."

"They maybe think you are bad medicine," Scarface said.

"Not when I give new rifle to each who join me," Red Dog said.

Nash chuckled. "It was somethin', wasn't it, that trader comin' all the way out here? What was he thinkin', the fool?"

"Him think to stop it," Red Dog said. "I get plenty more rifles now."

"So long as you have money to pay," Scarface said.

Their horses were on the other side of them, dozing. The wind was blowing from the animals to Fargo, so he wasn't worried they would catch his scent. He crept forward.

"A few months and we'll be right where we were," Nash declared happily. "All he's done is to be an inconvenience."

Red Dog snorted.

"It could be months before the army hears about McKindrick," Nash said. "And even when they do—" He stopped and raised his head. "Did you gents hear somethin'?"

"Only you. You talk too much," Red Dog said.

"I thought we were pards," Nash said.

Red Dog said, "You white-eye dog."

Scarface laughed.

Fargo quietly rose, leveled the Henry, and walked into the firelight.

26

Nash reached for his six-shooter but thought better of it and froze with his fingers splayed.

Scarface started to stand, but he, too, froze, scowling in anger.

Red Dog was as calm as could be. He didn't move except to slowly smile.

"Save any coffee for me?" Fargo said.

"Damn you to hell," Nash spat. "How did you find us?"

Fargo sidled to the right so he had clear shots at all three. "I followed his tracks," he said, and nodded at the Chiricahua.

Nash glanced at Red Dog. "What the hell? You didn't think to make it so he couldn't?"

"Him Fargo," Red Dog said. "Him good tracker."

"That's no answer," Nash said. "You could have doubled back a few times. Ridden across rocky country. You're an Apache, for God's sake. You know how to lose people followin' you."

Scarface was staring at Red Dog with a peculiar expression. "I thought we were friends."

"Need you once to get them," Red Dog said. "Not need you now."

Both Scarface and Nash looked as if they were about to throw themselves at him.

"Enough," Fargo said. He commanded Nash to unbuckle his gun belt and toss it. Muttering, the outlaw complied, throwing it just out of reach.

Fargo trained his Henry on Scarface, who had a knife on his hip and a revolver wedged under his belt. He had him shed them, one at a time.

That left Red Dog. His Henry was propped against his leg, the barrel on his knee. He'd made no attempt to resort to it and was still strangely calm.

"Your turn," Fargo said.

Smiling, Red Dog used two fingers to take the rifle by the barrel and slide it away from him. "Not yet," he said in his own tongue.

"Not yet what?" Fargo asked.

Red Dog went on smiling.

"So, now what?" Nash asked. "You haul us to the law? In case you forgot, there ain't any out here. It's every man for himself."

"Then here's no need to haul you anywhere," Fargo said, and pointed the Henry at him.

"Hold on!" Nash bleated, thrusting a hand out. "You can't blow out my wick like this."

"Why not?" Fargo said. "How many folks have you murdered, you miserable son of a bitch?"

Nash licked his lips. "I can tell you stuff. Stuff the army might like to know."

"Nash," Scarface said.

"About the rifles," Nash said. "The Henrys, and how the Apaches get their hands on them."

"Nash," Scarface said again, harshly.

"It all right," Red Dog said. "Let white-eye talk. Soon be over."

"Over for you, maybe," Nash said. "But not for me. I'll strike a deal with the army. In return for them lettin' me go, I'll testify at the trial."

"Against me?" Scarface said.

"Hell no. We were what the whites call the middle men. All we did was put them in touch with each other. We never bought or sold guns."

Fargo thought he understood. "Let me see if I have it figured out," he said. "Red Dog wanted repeaters. He couldn't get them himself. No white would trust him. So he went to Scarface and asked if Scarface knew any whites who'd be willing to sell rifles to him, and Scarface and you went to Abe McKindrick."

"McKindrick? We'd have been wastin' our breath. He'd never do somethin' illegal."

"But the Henrys came through his trading post," Fargo said. "I saw Red Dog there with my own eyes."

"That they did," Nash said. "He was there to pick up a few."

"Then who else but McKin—" Fargo stopped.

Nash laughed. "It was done right under McKindrick's nose. He caught on after you spoiled Red Dog's visit to the post, and it got him killed."

Scarface scowled. "You tell him too much."

"It's nothin' I wouldn't say at the trial," Nash said. "And it shows him that we're not the ones behind it."

"Damn," Fargo said.

"The light dawns," Nash said, and smirked. "So haul me in if you want. It won't be me they throw behind bars or hang."

Red Dog said quietly, "Him not haul anyone."

Fargo fixed a bead on the center of the Apache's chest. "Try something."

Red Dog didn't so much as blink. "How you like your horse, white-eye?"

Fargo raised his head. "My what?"

"You have good horse," Red Dog said. "Strong horse. Go far, not tire."

Fargo almost glanced up the canyon. But he didn't dare take his eyes off them.

"Horse ever go lame?" Red Dog asked.

"Why in hell are we talking about my horse?" Fargo said. He noticed that Scarface and Nash were as puzzled as he was.

"Horses go lame," Red Dog said.

"Now and then," Fargo said.

"What white-eye do when horse go lame? Shoot it?"

"Most whites care about their horses," Fargo said. "We don't shoot them unless it's to put them out of their misery."

"Not Shis-Inday," Red Dog said. "Horse go lame, Shis-Inday eat horse."

Fargo was well aware that Apaches never let themselves become too attached to their mounts. "I'd never eat mine."

"Warrior we call Long Knife have horse go lame," Red Dog related. "We cut throat, eat it." Then he said in his own tongue, "Do it now."

"Do what now?" Fargo said, unsure where this was leading.

"When white-eye horse die, white-eye ride with other white-eye," Red Dog said. "When Shis-Inday horse die, Shis-Inday use feet."

Fargo was also aware that Apache endurance put most others to shame.

"Long Knife follow," Red Dog said. "Him on foot so he fall behind."

"Is there a point to this?"

"Long Knife not at cliff," Red Dog said. "Me go to him after fight. Have him ride with me. Have him get off before me sit at fire. Have him wait in dark. Now him behind you."

Fargo stiffened and tried to turn but a sharp prick at the base of his neck dissuaded him.

Red Dog's smile widened. "You think you catch me, eh? Me catch you."

Nash laughed heartily. "I'll be damned. That was mighty slick. Scarface and me had no idea your friend was out there."

Scarface didn't take his eyes off Red Dog. Without saying a word he began to slide back from the fire.

"Where are you goin'?" Nash asked.

Suddenly Red Dog moved. In a heartbeat he had his Henry in his hands. He spun toward Scarface, and Scarface bolted into the night. The Henry boomed and there was a cry and a thud.

"What the hell?" Nash said.

Red Dog turned to him. "You not hear me say not need you anymore?"

Nash blanched. "Hold on. We did you a favor, set things up so you could get repeaters."

"You want money," Red Dog said. "Each time me buy rifles, you want money."

"Only our fair cut," Nash said. "It's how whites do things."

"It not how me do things," Red Dog said, and shot him in the face. Going over, he kicked the body and spat on it.

"White-eyes all same." He looked at Fargo. "You savvy why me kill him?"

Fargo nodded. Scarface and Nash had brokered the deal for the repeaters but Red Dog no longer needed them.

Red Dog came over and relieved Fargo of his Henry and the Colt. He backed up and dropped them and said in his own language, "Watch him, Long Knife. If he moves take his life."

"I will," Long knife said, and gouged the tip of his blade deeper.

Red Dog fell into a crouch, drew his own knife, and went beyond the firelight.

Fargo was under no illusions about why Red Dog wanted him alive. It would be Abner Pederson again, only worse, because there was no one to save him as he had saved Pederson.

From out of the dark came another cry and the sounds of a short scuffle. Red Dog reappeared, dragging Scarface by his hair. His knife dripped blood. Red Dog brought Scarface to the fire and without any forewarning whatsoever, he shoved Scarface's face into the flames. Scarface shrieked and weakly sought to resist and Red Dog slapped his hand away. Then, grinning viciously, Red Dog rolled him from the fire and flipped him roughly onto his back. "That only start," he said.

"I should think you'd be friendlier," Fargo said. "Him being part Indian."

"Him part white-eye," Red Dog spat. "Me hate breeds as much as hate whites."

Fargo was racking his brain for a way to get the better of them. All it would take was a flick of Long Knife's blade and his wandering days were over.

"Now time you die," Red Dog said.

"Hold on," Fargo said in an attempt to stall. "There's something I'd like to know first. How did you pay for the repeaters?"

"With money we take from white-eyes we kill," Red Dog answered.

Fargo had an inspiration. "You'll need more," he said. "A lot more if you want to buy repeaters for all your warriors."

"Me buy," Red Dog said, and thumped his chest. "Kill plenty whites and have plenty money."

"I have some."

Red Dog cocked his head.

"In my poke under my shirt," Fargo said.

"How much you have?"

Fargo pulled a figure out of thin air. "Three hundred and fifty-seven dollars." Truth was, he had about ten dollars to his name.

"Heap money," Red Dog said.

"Poker winnings," Fargo said. "How about I give it to you and you let me go free?"

Red Dog held his bloody knife poised to stab. "How about me take poke and cut out your heart?"

27

"You give me poke," Red Dog demanded. "You give me poke now."

"I reckon you don't leave me any choice," Fargo said, and went to reach inside his buckskin shirt. The pressure on the back of his neck lessened a little. It was all the opening he needed.

Lunging, Fargo grabbed Red Dog's wrist and pulled even as he drove his right boot back at Long Knife's leg. Red Dog was jerked off balance and Long Knife yelped. In a bound Fargo was in the darkness.

Fargo headed west but only a short way. Turning north, he went about ten strides and dropped flat.

Red Dog and Little Knife were after him. They came within a few dozen feet and kept going. When their footsteps faded, he heaved upright and sped toward the fire. They'd left his Henry and the Colt lying on the ground.

Scarface was struggling to rise. He'd been shot and stabbed and burned, but he had enough strength to make it to his knees. He saw Fargo burst into the light and grabbed at Fargo's Henry. He wrapped his fingers around it and was turning when Fargo reached him.

"Not today," Fargo said, and kicked him in the mouth. Scarface fell. Fargo tore the Henry from his grasp. Scarface sought to rise and Fargo smashed the stock against his forehead.

Moccasins slapped the earth.

Fargo whirled as Long Knife flew at him, the blade glinting in the firelight. Fargo fired from the hip. At the blast Long Knife was knocked half around but the shot hardly fazed him. With a fierce whoop, Long Knife came at him again. Fargo shot him in the forehead.

He had no time to congratulate himself. A shoulder caught him low in the back and he was slammed to the ground. He lost the Henry and glimpsed Red Dog diving for it.

The Colt was only a few feet away. Fargo pushed up, threw himself forward. He had it in his hand and twisted at the same instant that Red Dog turned with the Henry. They both fired, but Red Dog rushed his shot. Fargo fanned three swift shots, stitching holes from Red Dog's navel to his sternum.

Red Dog looked down at himself, said, "Me hate white-eyes." And died.

Fargo sank onto his back. He sucked in a breath, grateful to be alive.

It wasn't over, though.

"There's one more," he said out loud.

A week and a half went by before Fargo saw Cemetery again. He did a lot in that time.

The sun had relinquished the sky when he drew rein at the saloon. He went in and told the bartender he wanted Monongahela and downed the whiskey in a gulp.

"Where have you been?" the man asked. "The last I heard, you went off into the mountains after those Apaches."

"Mary McKindrick," Fargo said. "Is she still around?"

"Why wouldn't she be?" the man said. "Didn't you hear? Her husband disappeared and she's taken over the trading post and is running it herself."

"Do tell," Fargo said.

"She doing a right fine job, too. She's over there now, in fact. She usually works late just like McKindrick used to do."

Fargo paid and went out. He stood in the rectangle of light from the doorway and took off his hat and put it on again. It was the signal. Crossing to the trading post, he moved along the side of the building and checked the side door. It wasn't locked. He quietly opened it an inch or so, then returned to the front and went in by the front door.

Mary was behind the counter, humming to herself and writing in an account book.

Fargo made no noise until he was close enough to reach out and touch her. He stopped and coughed.

Mary gave a mild start. "Skye!" she exclaimed in delight. Rushing around the end of the counter, she threw her arms around him and hugged him tight. "You're alive! Where did you get to? I've been worried sick."

"Have you?"

Mary kissed him and laughed. "Why, this just about makes everything perfect."

"Does it?"

"I'm running the post now," Mary said, and gestured. "All I needed to make my life complete is you. And here you are." She kissed him a third time, heatedly.

Fargo leaned against the counter. "How soon before you sell everything and move back East?"

"I'm going to hold off on moving for a spell."

"I recollect you wanted to do that more than anything," Fargo mentioned. "As awful as your marriage was."

"But don't you see? Abner disappeared. Now all this is mine. The money I make is for me."

"Let me guess," Fargo said. "You hope to keep selling repeaters to the Apaches and save up until you have enough to live in grand style."

Mary went rigid.

"It'll be hard to do with Red Dog and Scarface dead," Fargo said. "But I reckon if you put your mind to it, you'll find another Apache to buy the guns."

Mary clasped her hands at her waist and regarded him coldly. "What a terrible thing to say to me." Wheeling, she went back around the counter. "I'd like you to leave now."

Fargo extended his arm as if to cup her breast, saying, "How about one for the road?"

"Don't you dare," Mary said, and took a step back. "After those preposterous accusations, do you honestly think I'd make love to you?"

"I buried him," Fargo said.

"Excuse me?"

"Abe. Your late, lamented husband. I buried what was left of him after Red Dog got through."

"You did?" Mary said, and swallowed.

"Did you watch? Did you laugh as he was being tortured?"

Mary colored and raised a hand as if to slap him but didn't. "You're despicable. I want you out of here."

"Abe told me everything," Fargo lied. "How it was you selling repeaters to the Apaches and not him. How when he found out he tried to stop it. He rode out to keep you from meeting with Red Dog and was caught."

Mary bit her bottom lip.

Fargo shrugged. "So I figured you must have watched." He paused. "I know Scarface was your go-between with Red Dog. What I don't savvy is how he knew to come to you and not your husband."

Mary came close to the counter. "I thought Abe told you everything." Her right hand slipped under it. "Nash and Scarface came to Abe. But he surprised me. He refused to sell rifles to them. He said he liked money as much as the next man, but he wouldn't sell repeaters that would be used to kill women and children."

"Imagine that."

"He didn't know I was listening. I'd come over to ask him what he wanted for supper and overheard everything. I slipped out real quick and went around to the side and when Nash and Scarface came out, I made the deal that Abe wouldn't."

"Ah," Fargo said.

"Don't you see? I wanted out. I wanted away from this place. I wanted it desperately. And they said Red Dog was willing to pay a lot of money."

"Where did you get the rifles? The army suspected Abe, but they investigated and it wasn't him."

Mary smiled slyly. "We went to Kansas City now and then to meet with suppliers. Abe told me that one of the men who sold rifles to him on occasion had a reputation for shady dealings. I wrote the man and he came for a visit and we struck a deal of our own."

"Did it include going to bed with him?"

"That's none of your business."

"One last question and then I'll pretty much have it all," Fargo said. "The night Red Dog was here and I swapped shots with him and his warriors. He came to pick up Henrys you'd gotten for him."

"You almost spoiled everything."

Fargo looked her in the eye. "It doesn't bother you in the least, does it?"

"Selling rifles to Apaches? No. Why should it? I don't know the people they kill. Or did you mean about Abe? No, again. He was a slug. He was no good in bed. He was no good for anything except making money."

"And now you don't need him for that."

"Red Dog and Scarface?" Mary said. "Are they really dead?"

"I killed the bastards myself."

"Well," Mary said. "I'm sure there must be other Apaches who want repeaters as much as Red Dog did. All I have to do is find someone who can go talk to them."

"You're forgetting about me," Fargo said. "I won't let you sell any more."

Mary's hand rose from under the counter holding a short-barreled Colt. She cocked it. "I'm afraid you can't stop me."

"The bartender will hear the shot. He'll run over."

"I'll tell him you tried to have your way with me," Mary said, "and I had to shoot you in self-defense." She pointed the Colt at his face. "Any last words?"

"I have to hand it to you. You pulled the wool over my eyes. I never suspected a thing."

"You were too busy lusting after my body." Mary grinned. "Not that I minded. You're about the handsomest man I ever made love to. It's a shame I have to blow that handsome face half off."

"It's not too late to hand me that revolver and turn yourself in."

Mary laughed. "Are you insane? Why would I do that? I have the upper hand."

"Then I guess we're done."

"I guess we are. I'm sorry. You shouldn't have poked your nose in."

"I'm sorry, too," Fargo said.

"About what?"

"About reporting you to the army. They asked me to help them track down the wretch who was selling the repeaters."

"You did no such thing."

Fargo raised his voice. "Come on in, gents. I trust you heard enough?"

An army officer and a stocky man with a tin star on his vest came in the side door. At the same time several soldiers came in the front, all of them with rifles they trained on Mary.

"I'd like you to meet Captain Bascomb and Marshal Reese," Fargo said. "The marshal is going to take you into custody and the army will press charges."

Mary had drained of all color. "No," she said.

"I'm afraid so, ma'am," Marshal Reese said. His hand was on his six-gun. "I'll have to ask you to set that pistol down."

Mary let go and the Colt clattered to the floor. She grabbed Fargo's arm and put her face close to his. "Please," she whispered. "Don't let them take me. I'll do anything. Anything at all. You can have my body every night for as long as you want me."

Fargo pried her fingers off. "There are a lot of other tits in this world." He smiled, touched his hat brim, and walked out and over to the saloon to get good and drunk.

LOOKING FORWARD!
The following is the opening
section of the next novel in the exciting
Trailsman series from Signet:

TRAILSMAN #371
CALIFORNIA KILLERS

1861, northern California—in the grip of a deadly drought, and someone is on a killing spree.

The first thing he felt was pain. Far above him was a faint light, and he was vaguely aware of sounds. He struggled to break through the pain and reach the light but a great blackness swallowed him.

How much time passed, he couldn't say. The pain brought him around again. It was duller, but it was everywhere. The light was back, too. It was closer. Again he struggled. It was like wading through black mud. He struggled for a long while, until the blackness claimed him as it had before.

The third time, the light was so close he could reach out and touch it. The pain was worse. He heard a creaking noise, and a *click-click-click*.

He was on his back and he was covered to his chin. He was naked from the waist up but he could tell he had pants on. He lay still, trying to make sense of where he was and how he got there. The clicking went on and he cracked his eyelids.

He was in a bed. His hands were folded on his chest. A blue blanket was over him, and he could see his feet poking up at the bottom.

Something was on his head. It was tight and most of the pain came from under it.

The creaking and the clicking continued. He swiveled his eyes. Something so simple, yet it hurt like hell.

A woman sat in a rocking chair, knitting. The creaking was the chair and the clicking was her needles. She appeared to be making a shawl. She wore a look of deep concentration as her fingers moved with practiced skill.

He wondered who she was. He searched his memory but there was nothing, nothing at all.

She was about thirty years old, he guessed. She had a nice face, not beautiful but nice. High cheekbones, a strong chin, full lips and green eyes, with light brown hair parted in the middle that hung to her shoulders. Her dress was home-spun.

The bedroom was plainly furnished. Besides the bed and the rocker, there was a small table next to the bed and a dresser over against the wall and another chair in the corner. A closet door hung open. Another door revealed a hallway. Curtains covered a window. The amount of light told him the sun was up.

He figured he should say something. His throat was so dry that when he tried, he couldn't. He had to swallow a few times. Finally he was able to croak, "Ma'am?"

She gave a mild start. She glanced at him, then stood and set her knitting on the rocker and came over. She put a warm palm to his forehead. "How do you feel?"

"Not so good," he admitted, and licked his lips. "Any chance of getting some water?"

"Certainly. I'll be right back."

She bustled out of the room. He lay quiet, collecting his thoughts, trying to remember how he got there. Doing that hurt, too.

Presently she returned with a pitcher of water and a glass. She filled the glass and set the pitcher on the small table. Sitting beside him, she carefully tilted the glass to his mouth.

He swallowed gratefully.

"More?"

He grunted.

"Let me know when you've had enough."

He drank the whole glass and felt considerably refreshed. "I'm obliged."

She set the glass by the pitcher and folded her hands on her knee. "To tell the truth, I didn't know if you'd ever come around. I'm no sawbones."

"Where am I?"

"My farm. My house. I have a hundred and sixty acres. It's not a lot but it's mine."

He eased a hand out from under the blanket and gingerly raised it to his head. Fully half the right side was bandaged.

"I did the best I could," she said. "I had to cut some of your hair to see how bad it was." She paused. "At least I didn't have to dig out a slug."

"I was shot?"

"You don't remember?"

He tried and admitted, "I don't recollect much of anything."

"You were shot," she confirmed. "I wouldn't have found you except for Skipper. She got out of the barn and I went searching for her and found her grazing near where you were lying."

"Skipper's your horse?"

"One of my milk cows. She's as contrary as anything and is always slipping off."

He had other questions he wanted to ask but the blackness was rising to devour him. He fought it. He tried to stay conscious. "No," he said, and was sucked under.

He came awake quickly. As always, the pain was there. The curtains were dark; it was night. The rocker was empty. He was the only one in the room.

Sliding his elbows under him, he managed to ease up. The effort cost him. He grew weak and the pain grew worse.

His head wound, he realized, must be a bad one.

The pitcher and the glass were still on the table. He had to try three times to reach for the pitcher, and then he couldn't lift it.

"God, I'm puny," he said to himself. It made him angry. He was a big man. He sensed that usually he was as strong as a bull.

He was determined. He gritted his teeth and raised the pitcher. It wobbled, and he nearly spilled it, but he managed to half fill the glass and set the pitcher down.

The glass was easier to lift.

He sat sipping, and thinking. He knew so little. It bothered him. He finished the water and put the glass by the pitcher.

The farmhouse was quiet. Somewhere a clock ticked. He debated calling out for the woman but she must be asleep.

He decided to try to get out of bed on his own. He rose higher, grimacing from the pain, and slowly slid his legs toward the edge. Agony lanced his head and his ears pounded with pressure.

He hated being so helpless. He straightened his legs and sank back and listened to the clock. Who was the woman? He didn't know. Where was he? He didn't know.

He wearily closed his eyes, not intending to doze off, but he did.

Sunlight filled the bedroom.

The creaking and the clicking were back. He looked at her and smiled and said, "Morning."

"Good afternoon, you mean," she said, coming over. "It's pretty near two. You slept the whole night away, and then some. But you needed it."

"I recollect having some water."

"Would you like more?"

"What I'd like is food," he said, and his stomach rumbled in agreement.

"Oh. Of course." She went to the doorway, and paused. "Before I forget, I reckon I should introduce myself. I'm Marabeth Arden." She smiled, and was gone.

He liked her name, Marabeth. He liked her. That she had gone to so much trouble on his behalf touched him. Some people wouldn't have bothered.

He liked her farmhouse, too. The feel of it. The quiet. The ticking of the clock. It occurred to him that a man could get used to something like this, and the thought seemed to startle him, although why, he couldn't say.

Aromas reached his nose. The food she was cooking. His mouth watered and his stomach wouldn't stop growling.

He was so famished that when Marabeth returned bearing a tray, he wanted to leap out of bed and take it from her and dig in.

"Here you go," she said. "It's not much. The best I could do on short order."

Her "not much" consisted of eggs and bacon and toast smeared with strawberry jam. She'd also brought a cup of steaming hot coffee. She placed the tray in his lap and sat so close, their shoulders brushed. "I can feed you if you like."

"I'm not a baby," he said, and for some reason she frowned.

He picked up a fork and stabbed a piece of scrambled egg and put it in his mouth. He chewed slowly, and moaned. Never had food tasted so delicious. "Thank the chicken for me," he said.

Marabeth laughed. "My hens will be happy to hear their laying is appreciated. I tend to take them for granted, I'm afraid."

He grinned, and helped himself to some bacon, and swore he was in heaven.

"I never saw anyone who likes to eat so much."

"I'm starved." He bit off a piece of toast. The jam was the best he'd ever tasted.

"You didn't hear anything outside last night, did you?" Marabeth asked unexpectedly.

"No, ma'am," he said. "I was out to the world. Why?"

She shrugged. "Just curious. I thought I might have."

He went on eating. Every last bit of egg, every last crumb. He washed it down with the coffee and sat back. A feeling of sluggishness came over him but he didn't mind.

He put his hand on his washboard belly, and was content.

"Is there anything else I can get you?" Marabeth asked.

The words came out of his mouth before he could stop them. "I don't suppose you have any whiskey?"

"In your condition?" Marabeth said. "I don't know as that would be good for you. It might make your head worse, and you don't want that."

No, he didn't. "I'd settle for more coffee, then."

"I'll be right back." She took the tray with her.

He closed his eyes, and damn if he didn't fall asleep. When he opened them again she was in the rocking chair and the curtains were gray. "Not again," he said.

"I beg your pardon?"

"How long this time?"

"Five hours or so." Marabeth put down her knitting and came over. "You're looking better. There's color in your cheeks. When I found you, you were pale as a ghost. I thought maybe you'd bled to death, but when I checked for a pulse there was one."

"I'm in your debt."

She smiled, and in the soft light she was lovely. "I'd have done the same for anyone. Well, almost anyone." She paused. "So, tell me. Who are you? Who shot you? What were you doing there?"

He reached inside himself for the answers, but there was a blank slate. It couldn't be, and yet it was.

His shock must have shown.

"What's the matter?" Marabeth asked.

"I don't know who I am."